The DEMON SWORD MASTER of Excalibur Academy

REGINA

Riselia's maid, who's an expert at teasing people

ELFINÉ

A dependable upperclassman

SAKUYA

A girl hailing from the Sakura Orchid

LEONIS
The reincarnated Undead King and *strongest* **Dark Lord**

RISELIA
Leonis's *caretaker* **(?)**

"I can
wash
myself..."

"Sweep
everything,
flames
of
inferno,
and
reduce
all to
ashes..."

The
DEMON SWORD MASTER
of Excalibur Academy

Yu Shimizu

ILLUSTRATION
Asagi Tosaka

The DEMON SWORD MASTER of Excalibur Academy

[1]

Yu Shimizu

ILLUSTRATION

Asagi Tosaka

YEN ON
NEW YORK

The DEMON SWORD MASTER of Excalibur Academy

Yu Shimizu

Translation by Roman Lempert
Cover art by Asagi Tosaka

SEIKEN GAKUIN NO MAKEN TSUKAI Vol. 1
©Yu Shimizu, Asagi Tosaka 2019
First published in Japan in 2019 by KADOKAWA CORPORATION, Tokyo.
English translation rights arranged with KADOKAWA CORPORATION, Tokyo
through TUTTLE-MORI AGENCY, INC., Tokyo.

English translation © 2020 by Yen Press, LLC

Yen On
150 West 30th Street, 19th Floor
New York, NY 10001

Visit us at yenpress.com
facebook.com/yenpress ★ twitter.com/yenpress
yenpress.tumblr.com ★ instagram.com/yenpress

First Yen On Edition: August 2020

Yen On is an imprint of Yen Press, LLC.
The Yen On name and logo are trademarks of Yen Press, LLC.

The publisher is not responsible for websites (or their content) that are not owned by the publisher.

Library of Congress Cataloging-in-Publication Data
Names: Shimizu, Yu, author. | Tosaka, Asagi, illustrator. | Lempert, Roman, translator.
Title: The demon sword master of Excalibur Academy / Yu Shimizu ; illustration by Asagi Tosaka ; translation by Roman Lempert.
Other titles: Seiken gakuin no maken tsukai. English
Description: First Yen On edition. | New York : Yen On, 2020.
Identifiers: LCCN 2020017005 | ISBN 9781975308667 (v. 1 ; trade paperback)
Subjects: CYAC: Fantasy. | Demonology—Fiction. | Reincarnation—Fiction
Classification: LCC PZ7.1.S5174 De 2020 | DDC [Fic]—dc23
LC record available at https://lccn.loc.gov/2020017005

ISBNs: 978-1-9753-0866-7 (paperback)
978-1-9753-0867-4 (ebook)

1 3 5 7 9 10 8 6 4 2

LSC-C

Printed in the United States of America

Contents

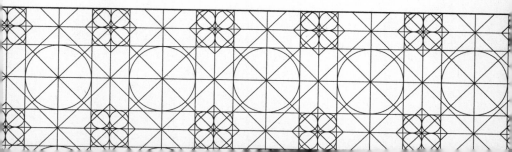

Year 447 of the Holy Calendar.

It was the age of myth, when gods, spirits, and magic ruled over the land. The war between the Dark Lords' Armies and the Six Heroes was approaching its conclusion.

Bones piled upon bones. The remains of countless skeletons littered the ground, blanketed by a heavy black smog.

"—And so my capital of Necrozoa, too, is destined to fall."

The Undead King, Leonis Death Magnus, sat upon a throne in the deepest recesses of the black fortress known as Death Hold. He sighed, exhaling a thick miasma. He was clad in a pitch-black robe cloaked with a smoky mist thick with curses and dark magic. His visage was as death incarnate and stood as a symbol of fear and awe for mankind.

At the moment, however, the Undead King's capital of Necrozoa and its dark lands were being overrun by an alliance of humans, demi-humans, and spirits. His realm was teetering on the edge of destruction.

The Six Heroes blessed by the gods had already attacked the other Dark Lords' fortresses across the land. The Crag Castle of

Dizolf, the Lord of Rage. The Ironblood Castle of Gazoth, the Lord of Beasts. The Otherworldly Castle of Azra-Ael, the Devil of the Underworld. The Demon Dragon's Mountain Range of Veira, the Dragon Lord. Even the Underwater Stronghold of Rivaiz, the Lord of the Seas. All of them had fallen.

The only bastion remaining was Necrozoa.

Through a crystal orb in his hand, the Undead King, Leonis, watched over the battle. The clattering sounds of bones clicking together rode the breeze across the field of battle. Countless skeleton soldiers created by Leonis's mana filled the wasteland. An army of the undead, impervious to swords or spears. But even this vast assemblage was being torn apart... The violence swept across the battlefield and left soldiers scattered like petals in the wind.

"The Six Heroes...!"

A massive tree bathed in shining light sprouted in the center of the battlefield. Its roots burst from the ground, blowing away the skeleton soldiers and crushing them to splinters.

"The Archsage Arakael. So even you have discarded your humanity. To think you would debase yourself to a servant of the gods...!" the Undead King whispered in annoyance, crushing the crystal orb in his grip.

Having accepted the gods' blessings into their bodies, the Six Heroes had gained the power to evolve without end. The wisest of the six—the Archsage Arakael—had consumed the Holy Tree, guardian of the Spirit Forest, and made its power his own.

"It's time I joined the battle. My dark flames shall feast on these fools."

The Undead King Leonis took up his staff and rose from his throne, his black robe swaying in his wake.

"Wait, Lord Magnus."

The Undead King turned to face the voice calling out from

behind him. A black wolf held the hem of his cloak in its mouth and looked up at Leonis. It was Blackas Shadow Prince, the prince of the Realm of Shadows and longtime comrade and friend to the Undead King.

"You are the last remaining Dark Lord. That one would not wish for you to fall here," he said, raising his gaze to meet Leonis's.

Leonis stopped in his tracks. His grip tightened around his staff.

"Yes...I suppose you're right."

Leonis remembered it well. The mission she—the Goddess of Rebellion—had bestowed upon him.

"In one thousand years' time, when stars fall from the heavens, a vessel for my power will appear in the form of a child of man."

Finding the goddess's vessel and re-forming the Dark Lords' Armies was his mission. The final mission given to the last remaining Dark Lord.

"Be content in knowing that I acknowledge my defeat this time, foolish humans. But I am the Undead King. A millennium from now, I will be reborn and reclaim this throne!"

—And so it was that the Undead King sealed his own soul in the depths of the Grand Mausoleum.

CHAPTER 1

THE UNDEAD KING AWAKENS

"—We're currently on the seventh stratum. No Void reactions detected."

"—ger. —up the...vestigation."

A reply mixed with static crackled back at the girl from her earring-type device. Holy Swordsmen candidates from Excalibur Academy often delved deep into the underground ruins, where regular military communication terminals were ineffective.

"Lady Selia, isn't it about time we withdraw?"

"Reports say they've built a nest deep beneath the ruins. We should search a bit farther."

The girl strode forward gallantly. Her long, silver hair fluttered behind her. The young woman's ice-blue eyes held an intense determination and were fixed straight ahead in a dignified expression.

The light of a rod-shaped magical device made her visible even in the darkness. She was fifteen years old, and her beautiful metallic hair reflected the rays of light. Her white skin was fair and sleek like a snow fairy's, and her lips were a light shade of pink.

Her appearance carried such grace that if she were to walk

through town, anyone would turn to get a better look at her. One could sense that noble blood ran through her veins.

Riselia Ray Crystalia.

In truth, she was a descendant of the nobles who supervised the Assault Gardens, and one normally wouldn't find a person of her social standing striding through such a dangerous place.

"Yes, yes. You're as diligent as ever, Lady Selia."

The response came with a wry smile and a shrug from a petite girl with blond hair tied into pigtails. Regina Mercedes was Riselia's personal maid. Her jasper eyes were lively and alert, and her limber, well-trained limbs granted her a certain beauty reminiscent of a wild animal.

Both of them wore the same navy-blue uniform. It was the official uniform worn by Holy Swordsmen of the Seventh Assault Garden's own Excalibur Academy. Their task was to investigate an ancient ruin that had suddenly appeared in a wasteland.

Several days ago, a large earthquake had occurred in the area, exposing the ruin. Ancient sites where mana gathered easily often became Void hives, and so they had been dispatched to investigate.

Reconnaissance missions like these were dangerous. And while the Canary Unit often made light of them, a mere six months earlier, a team on just such a run had encountered a group of Voids and had been wiped out.

The Voids.

They were invaders from another world. They had appeared sixty years ago and begun their offensive on human civilization, eradicating three-quarters of mankind. Everything about them was a mystery. Where had they come from? What was their objective? Even their biology was unclear. Were they weapons or living beings? No one knew. The only thing that was certain was that they took on forms resembling mythological creatures.

"It's an important duty. If we left a hive unchecked, it'd be the same as letting them invade the city…"

Riselia bit her lip and hastened her stride. She wasn't above being apprehensive about the situation. If anything, she was more easily frightened than most. It was why she always hid behind her older sister's back when she was younger.

The air in the underground ruin was tepid and reeked of mold. It was like a graveyard.

…It could actually be a graveyard, for all I know, Riselia thought.

This site was probably centuries old. Looking around, statues of what appeared to be fictional monsters were stationed here and there. Perhaps this was a grave for some king…

…It would probably have been a very strict king, Riselia mused.

The two walked through the silent corridor, wary of the potential presence of Voids. And then…

"…Aw, a dead end?" Regina frowned, stopping in her tracks.

"This…looks like a door…," Riselia said, looking up at the massive wall before her.

She tried shoving it with both hands, but no luck.

"Should I bust through?" Regina offered, suggesting something unspeakably hazardous.

"Wait, there's something written on it." Riselia stopped her.

She held up the rod, using it to illuminate the door. Letter-like marks were etched over it. Acquainted though she was with ancient ruins, Riselia had never seen anything like this writing.

"Can you read it?"

"Hmm, I think it's ancient Elvish…or maybe it's spirit text…?"

Riselia took out a small analysis device and began typing quickly.

"What's the matter?"

"—This door, it's still alive."

"Alive?"

"Its system is still operating. It's like an ancient magical apparatus..."

"I'll go keep watch, then." Regina shrugged, sighing.

She knew Riselia's personality well enough.

"Yeah, please."

Regina waved and went back down the corridor. She wasn't good with boredom. Taking independent action during a ruin investigation was reckless, but unlike Riselia, she had the power of a Void-slaying Holy Sword. She'd be fine.

Riselia worked on her analysis device and began deciphering the ancient letters. A similar text structure should exist in the database. Riselia wondered what could be beyond this barrier. She found herself surprisingly drawn to it. But the moment her fingers brushed against the inscription...

A spark of magical energy flashed.

"Huh...?"

Brrrrrrrrrrrrrrrrrrrrrrrrrrrrrrrrrrrrr...

The heavy stone door sluggishly opened before her.

"...It opened?!" Riselia's eyes widened as she illuminated the interior with her light.

What's that...?

Embedded into the rock was a massive, eerily luminescent black crystal the likes of which Riselia had never seen before. Her device let out a high-pitched warning sound.

A mana reaction...?

The mana-detecting tool was displaying errors.

It was a counter stop—a freeze in the program because a theoretically impossible figure had been input.

"Oh, come on—don't break on me now...," Riselia whispered as she approached the crystal.

As she did, she noticed a human figure inside it, sealed in darkness.

"...N-no way... How?!"

She held her breath for a moment and then peered into the crystal again. There really was someone trapped in there.

I have to save them...!

Riselia drew a pistol from her holster.

◆

Bang, bang, ba-bang!

...Why is it so loud...?

An unpleasant sound echoed outside the casket...

The Undead King—Leonis Death Magnus—stirred from sleep. He was in the Grand Mausoleum, located beneath the legendary undead capital of Necrozoa. Frozen time began to move, and the Undead King's soul, sealed within the casket, awoke.

Has it been a thousand years already...?

Bang, bang, bang!

As he peered into the darkness, thoughts began circulating through his mind. He had been entirely unconscious while sealed inside the casket. For him, time had not advanced since that day the undead army was defeated by the heroes of mankind and his capital of Necrozoa, the last fortress of his army, fell.

Bang, bang, bang!

It seems the ritual of reincarnation was successful...

Leonis tried clenching his fingers in the darkness. He was still a bit numb, but he could definitely feel his limbs. Even the Undead King couldn't maintain his body for a thousand years without a supply of mana. And so he had employed a secret art of undeath to suspend his soul and had used this casket to reincarnate his form—

Bang, bang, bang, bang!

...Grrrrrrrrr, I demand silence*!*

The Undead King Leonis practically shouted the thought, annoyed at having been consistently interrupted while he was thinking.

What is that noise anyway?

Apparently, someone was beating on his casket.

What manner of scoundrel would dare disturb the Undead King's slumber?

The Grand Mausoleum was sealed below the earth with a powerful barrier, so it was hard to imagine it could be easily discovered. It had been one thousand years, though, and there was no saying what manner of disaster or cataclysm could have struck in that time.

But the crypt was completely shut away by an anti-magic wall...

Leonis concentrated on the noise outside the casket. Whatever dastard was trying to destroy the casket was apparently saying something.

It seems to be the human tongue. Hmm...

After one thousand years, a language's syntax was bound to change somewhat. Extending his fingers into the darkness, he chanted a language analysis spell, and a light flashed before him. Even after reincarnation, this body of flesh was capable of using magic without any trouble.

"This can't be normal rock if it deflects bullets this easily. Guess I'll try an anti-material round next..."

He didn't quite understand everything they were saying, but it seemed they were out to destroy the casket.

...Foolish grave robbers, it seems, Leonis concluded.

It went without saying that his casket was impervious to most conventional forms of magic. Regardless, he would have to punish this scoundrel.

—Behold the revived form of the Undead King. Die with the image burned into your eyes!

Leonis extended his hand, and...

Crrrrrrrrrrrrack!

The dark-crystal casket shattered with an ear-numbing sound, loosing a powerful shock wave that knocked back the figure who had stood at Leonis's coffin.

"........."

Having been revived after a millennium of slumber, the Undead King looked around, lording over it all. The atmosphere of the underground Grand Mausoleum hadn't changed one bit. The air was completely still, thick with the presence of death.

"...Aah... Nnng...!"

Leonis's gaze fell to the person before him, who was crouched down and moaning in pain. The shock wave hadn't been his intended punishment for this insolent grave robber, of course. He would exact his vengeance starting now, and he planned to give them an ample taste of terror for the newly resurrected Undead King, and—

"...?!"

The moment he took a step forward, Leonis's eyes widened.

There was a source of light lying on the ground, illuminating the shape of...a girl. She looked to be fourteen or fifteen years old. Her hair was a shining shade of silver, and her eyes were ice blue. Her skin was the color of virgin snow. Overall, her beauty matched that of the high elves.

No... Have even the high elves ever known a girl of such beauty? Her loveliness was like the chiseled artistry of a goddess's statue. Watching her with a mystified look on his face, Leonis stood frozen, his breath held.

He needed to punish this brazen thief... But the thought evaporated like mist. The girl was wearing a kind of garb that Leonis had never seen before. It was like the uniform of a light cavalry soldier, except its basic tone was dark blue, and it had a skirt attached. Suffice to say, she certainly didn't look to be any kind of robber.

"Wh-what...?" She raised her voice, looking up at Leonis.

Rather than fear, her voice was full of surprise.

...*Right. I must hand down punishment...*

He cleared his throat, but then...

"...What... What's a kid doing here?" she asked.

"...Pardon?" Leonis returned with his own query despite himself. *What does she mean by "kid"...?*

Furrowing his brow, the Undead King looked down at his limbs.

"...What?!" His eyes widened in shock.

I-impossible...!

Small, undependable hands. Soft, unblemished skin. The physique beneath his black robe was like that of a small child... No, it wasn't *like* that of a child. The Undead King Leonis Death Magnus found himself inhabiting the form of a ten-year-old boy.

...*Could the ritual of reincarnation have failed somehow?!*

The spell of reincarnation was a twelfth-order spell of the highest caliber and had several variations to it.

One involved rebirth by transferring one's soul to another vessel. Another involved creating a new vessel by way of magic and fixing one's soul in it. Yet another was to return one's body to a past state and restructure it. That was the method Leonis had chosen.

He had elected to restore his damaged body to its prime, using that as the vessel for his soul. Not unlike a phoenix reborn from within the flames.

But why do I look like this...?

He had prepared the spell to restructure his body into that of the Undead King. So why had it reverted to this despicable shape—the form he'd had when he was still known as the Hero Leonis? His dark robe felt loose. Compared to the body he'd had when he was the Undead King, this one felt far less reliable.

"Erm..."

Apparently relieved that the one who appeared before her was a young boy, the silver-haired girl adjusted the hem of her skirt and slowly rose to her feet. She kneeled in front of Leonis and peered intently into his face before looking again at the shattered pieces of the dark-crystal casket.

"Why were you inside that thing?"

"...W-well, that's..."

With those ice-blue eyes gazing straight at him, his heart skipped a beat.

...Ugh, this is why I loathe the flesh of a human body...

"Did the Voids abduct you?" she asked.

"...Voids?" Leonis frowned. That was an unfamiliar word.

"...I see. Your memories must be jumbled because of the shock..."

And inspired by whatever unknown urge might've struck her, the young woman suddenly took Leonis's body in a tight embrace.

"...!"

"...Everything will be all right."

"Wh-what, what are you...?!"

"Your big sister will keep you safe."

"S-stop it... Mmm, nnng, mmmf!"

Squish.

The Undead King's face was being pressed against a pair of soft, supple fruits—the plump chest of a young woman. The tips of her silvery locks tickled his cheeks, and her dainty fingers gently brushed through his hair.

...!

This was quite a disrespectful manner with which to treat the Undead King who had reigned over the capital of Necrozoa. But for some reason, Leonis couldn't (or rather wouldn't) resist her hold on him. His heart was beating fast at these long-forgotten feelings he had once known as a human being. The sensation of her embrace was simply too pleasant.

...Huh...?

A sudden spell of dizziness came over him. Nestled in the soft, cushion-like embrace of a woman's bosom, the Undead King Leonis's consciousness sank into darkness...

◆

...Hmm, I see. These have dried grapes kneaded into them.

Sitting atop the stone altar of the Grand Mausoleum, Leonis was stuffing his face with the hard biscuits the silver-haired girl handed him.

They're reminiscent of the portable foodstuffs the elves would carry, except they were drier than these.

He'd discarded his sense of taste eons ago, but the experience of eating wasn't all that bad.

"...Mmm, nng, aagh..."

A lump of a biscuit got stuck in his throat, and Leonis started coughing and beating his chest.

This body truly is an incorrigible thing. To think I'd lose consciousness out of hunger..., Leonis thought, bitterly.

Yes, Leonis had fainted because of mere hunger... It was

actually quite dangerous. The strongest Dark Lord passing out because of an empty stomach was an unimaginable blunder.

He'd never dreamed he'd reincarnate into his human body, so he had prepared no food or water. He hated to admit it, but...

Leonis raised his head, looking at the girl sitting a short distance away from him.

...This woman may well have just saved my life.

Normally, this would be an accomplishment great enough to warrant awarding her the highest honor he could bequeath, the Bone Medal. Said girl had her hand pressed against her earring and seemed to be speaking to someone.

"I've discovered a child refugee in the ruin. Requesting confirmation."

"—Roger... I'll cross-reference the refugee lists."

It was some sort of long-distance communication magic. Perhaps the earring served as a kind of magic catalyst? The girl seemed to have noticed Leonis staring at her and gave him a relieved smile.

"Thank goodness. Is your tummy feeling better now?"

"........"

Leonis nodded wordlessly, prompting the girl to move next to him.

"My name is Riselia Crystalia. I'm a Holy Swordswoman of the Seventh Assault Garden's training academy, eighteenth platoon... Oh, um, I'm fifteen years old. What's your name?"

She diligently kept her gaze at Leonis's eye level and introduced herself. He technically understood her, but honestly, nothing she said seemed to register as meaningful to him. The only things Leonis really grasped were her name and age.

When it came to human-ruled nations in the area, the Lagard Kingdom and the Magocracy of Sheniebel came to mind, but the girl had not mentioned them insofar as he could tell. Also, this

Riselia seemed to be under the impression that Leonis was a child who'd been abducted by monsters.

...I suppose I cannot fault her for that, given the way I look, Leonis thought in a self-deprecating manner.

He didn't know what had caused his rebirth in this body... But he figured he might as well take advantage of the girl's misunderstanding.

...For now, I need to get information about this world out of her.

Leonis raised his head.

"I am... Erm, *I'm* Leonis. Leonis Magnus, Miss."

He tried to make his voice a bit more high-pitched to seem more childlike, but he still gave his name as a Dark Lord. He'd considered using a pseudonym, but going to such lengths with mere humans would wound his pride as a Dark Lord.

Besides, this was the proud name *she* had given him.

How will this one react to it...?

If the name of Leonis Death Magnus, the Undead King, was recorded in legend and passed down for posterity, it should elicit some kind of reaction from the girl.

"Leonis?" The girl's light-blue eyes widened.

Ooh, so she does know of—

"What a cute name!"

"...R-really?" Leonis said with a grimace.

...What could possibly be cute about it? It was a name that struck terror into every corner of the world!

Evidently, his reputation as a Dark Lord hadn't survived these many years.

"Leonis...Leo, how old are you?" Riselia asked.

"Ten years old...or so," he replied, holding back the urge to snap at her for shortening the name of a Dark Lord.

"Or so?"

"Ah, I'm ten years old."

He no longer remembered how old he'd been before becoming the Undead King. But it was probably close enough.

"You're a refugee, right? Do you remember what the Void that took you looked like?"

"Void?" Leonis parroted the word.

"You don't know what Voids are?"

"Erm...no."

"Right... I suppose that does happen out in the frontier regions," Riselia placed a hand on her chin and nodded, seemingly convinced. "Voids are enemies of mankind. They came here from another world. The Holy Swordsmen—that is to say, us—fight those Voids."

"...Other world? Enemies?" Leonis was rather confused.

One thousand years ago, the ones called "enemies of mankind" had been the demons and the Dark Lords' Armies. Alongside them was the Goddess of Rebellion, who'd betrayed the other deities of the Luminous Powers and declared war upon the world.

Have new forces risen in the world over the last thousand years? But...

The goddess's prophecy had said nothing of this.

"We came to investigate a Void hive that's formed in these ruins. They tend to show up around places like these. And..."

Riselia turned to look at the opened door of the mausoleum.

"That's when I found this door."

Now Leonis understood. She'd only found this place by way of coincidence. He couldn't honestly say he much liked the idea of her unlocking the sealed door, but perhaps it had opened because one of the Undead King's servants had rigged it to do so after one thousand years.

No, wait...

Leonis realized he'd neglected to confirm something terribly important.

"Erm...Miss Riselia?"

"You can call me Selia, Leo."

"Then, uhhh, Miss Selia. What year of the Holy Calendar is it?"

He had asked using the calendar employed by human nations. If it'd been one thousand years since Necrozoa, the final stronghold of the Dark Lords' Armies, had fallen, the year should have been around 1447. However...

"Holy Calendar?" Riselia gave a quizzical expression and furrowed her brow. "It's the sixty-fourth year of the Integrated Human Calendar..."

"Integrated Human Calendar?" This time it was Leonis's turn to parrot Riselia.

Another unfamiliar term.

...Just what in the world is going on?

It was then that Riselia's earring lit up.

"—ady Selia...careful...engaged in battle...large Void..."

"Huh? What, Regina?!"

The voice filled with static before cutting off.

"What's the matter?"

"...I'm not sure. But—" Riselia got to her feet with a sharp expression.

And the next moment...

Booooooooooooooooooooom!

Beneath Necrozoa, the Grand Mausoleum shook violently.

◆

"Wh-what?!"

Pebbles and fragments of stone began crumbling down on them from the ceiling. Riselia reflexively covered Leonis to shield him.

...!

A soft chest pressed against his face from beneath a uniform.

"Are you okay, Leo?"

"...Y-yes..." Leonis nodded, feeling his pulse quicken.

The scent of a young woman's sweat lingered in his nostrils.

"It seems a Void's shown up. My friend's fighting it." Riselia released him and looked around cautiously.

Bang, bang, bang!

Intermittent explosions could be heard from the distance.

...Ugh, how dare they run amok in this tomb, the resting place of my comrades...?!

As the Dark Lord of Necrozoa, he couldn't permit such disregard. Leonis tried to rise to his feet—

"...Whoa!"

"Leo?!"

—but tripped over the cuffs of his long robe and fell forward.

C-curses...

Rubbing his aching nose, this time he got up slowly. He wasn't used to his boyish body yet.

"Are you all right? You're not hurt, are you?"

"I-I'm fine."

"You're a tough little guy, aren't you?" Riselia smiled with relief and patted Leonis on the head.

...It tickled. But Leonis was surprised to find it wasn't unpleasant.

Really, what in the world is going on...?

"Don't worry. I'll keep you safe." Riselia stood and drew a metallic lump from a belt tied around her hip.

"Artificial Relic, Ray Hawk. Limited Initialization...Activate!" the girl whispered, holding the object in both hands.

The lump made a kind of loud clicking sound and changed its shape. What was now in the girl's grasp was a cylindrical object that shined with a mana flare. It was probably some kind of projectile weapon, though nothing like it had existed in Leonis's time.

"Over here..." Riselia took Leonis by the hand and broke into a run.

The next moment...

Baaaaaaaaaaaaaaaaaaaaaaang!

"...?!"

A massive fist broke through the ruin's wall.

"An ogre-class Void?!" Riselia exclaimed, her expression tense.

Did she just say "ogre"?!

Tension rose in Leonis at the first familiar word he'd heard today. Ogres—they were a race of man-eating demons that was part of the Dark Lords' Armies under the command of the Lord of Rage, Dizolf. Leonis soon found his expectations dashed, however.

"Leo, get back...!"

What stepped through the collapsed wall was a giant standing five meters tall. What appeared to be luminescent red minerals grew out of its gray body. Nothing on its head gave the impression of being an eye, and it only had a horizontal opening across its face to serve as an eerie sort of mouth. Its drooping arms were covered in scales, and what looked like a beastly face writhed across its chest.

How is this an ogre...?

This was as far-removed as could be from the ogres Leonis knew. If it reminded him of anything, it was the disgusting hybrid creatures that Zemein, a staff officer in the Dark Lords' Armies, had once worked on. Leonis and Zemein had rarely seen eye to eye.

"That's a Void?!"

At his question, Selia glared at the monster and nodded in

reply. "Yes. An enemy of humanity that takes the form of the gods of old—"

Pop! A dry, bursting sound rang out. Riselia had likely fired her projectile weapon, but it didn't seem to have any effect. The creature's scales deflected the shot.

"...Ugh, this weapon can't even make a dent...!"

"■■■■■■■■■■!"

The Void roared from its horrific mouth, exhaling a dark smoke from the eerie oral cavity. It twisted its drooping arms like whips, sweeping Riselia back.

"Hmph. Ri Larte...!"

Leonis started chanting a spell from the Realm of Shadows to form a barrier when suddenly—

Boom! Boom! Boom!

—a series of intermittent explosions shook his eardrums. Crimson flames blew off the Void's right arm, leaving bursts of hot air in their wake.

"Are you all right, Lady Selia?!"

"...Regina!"

The one who had fired through the wall to reach them was a petite girl carrying a giant cylindrical weapon. Her golden hair was parted into pigtails, which danced in the intense rush of air from the blasts...

As an aside, her chest was also prodigious.

Her jasper-colored eyes shone, catlike in the darkness. Her features were quite fair as well, not unlike Riselia's.

She used the blast's momentum to slide over the ground, halting with a screech.

"Like we thought, this ruin is a Void spawn point... Wait. Lady Selia, who's the kid?" The girl called Regina looked at Leonis and cocked her head in surprise.

"I found him deep in the ruins. I'll explain later..."

"Right..."

"■■■■■■■■■■!"

The monster got up, shaking off pieces of rubble as it did. Its right arm, which had just been blown off, had already begun to regenerate. The creature's vitality was truly fearsome.

"That's a large class for you. This much firepower won't get us anywhere..." Regina fixed her grip on the massive projectile launcher on her shoulder. "Holy Sword Drag Howl, Mode Shift—

"The Anti-Large Aerial Beast Extermination Weapon—Dragon Slayer!"

And the next moment, the bulky weapon changed. Its muzzle took the form of a dragon's maw, gaping even wider...

...*What in the world is this device...?!*

Leonis's eyes widened.

Do you mean to say...that's a Holy Sword?

"Get smooooked!"

Booooooooooooooooooooooom!

A shell burst forward. A white flash filled Leonis's field of vision, followed by a rumbling blast.

...*M-my poor Grand Mausoleum!*

Leonis had to hold back from saying the words out loud. Even so, the weapon's power was incredible. The sheer amount of heat it produced was equivalent to that of the fourth-order explosion-type magic, Rag Illa.

But that isn't magic.

He hadn't seen a mana flare, which magic always produced when it was invoked.

"D-did you finish it off?"

"Erm, Lady Selia, what you just did is called jinxing it..."

They could see its colossal shadow slowly rising from beyond the cloud of dust.

Oh? So it can even take an attack with the firepower of a Rag Illa spell...

Leonis was impressed. Most demons would be reduced to dust from that much. The blond girl stepped forward, glaring at the figure beyond the dust.

"Leave the ruin, you two. I'll take care of this..."

"Regina..." Riselia hesitated for a moment, but then nodded. "All right. Be careful."

"I will, Lady Selia." Regina smiled at her.

The briefness of this exchange made the trust between the two of them evident.

"Let's go, Leo." Riselia grabbed Leonis by the arm and took off.

◆

It's one unexpected thing after another..., Leonis thought as he let her pull him away.

Shouldn't a Dark Lord's revival be a more solemn, dignified affair?

He'd (quite obviously) failed at the reincarnation ritual, instead returning to an incarnation of the boy he had been before becoming the Undead King. His crypt was infested with these otherworldly Void creatures, and the place was being wrecked without regard for its master's—his—will.

He wanted nothing more than to turn around and give that monster what was coming to it, but he couldn't afford to do that. Leonis snuck a glance at Riselia's face as she ran ahead of him. The girl was an important source of information, and so he had to keep his identity as the Undead King hidden if he was to learn anything more.

"Let's head for the surface, okay?" Riselia asked, panting all the while.

...There's a shortcut to the surface, though.

However, pointing that out could raise the girl's suspicions.

"...Ah!"

Suddenly feeling a presence, Leonis reflexively tugged on Riselia's sleeve.

Boooooooooooooooooom!

The ruin's ceiling caved in. Had the two walked any farther, they'd have surely been crushed under the rubble.

"...Leo...?"

"It looks like there was more than just one of them."

Leonis turned his back to Riselia, who had fallen behind him, and looked ahead. A massive, winged shadow looked down on them from beyond the dust.

"...Not another one!"

"Is that a Void, too?"

"Yes, a flying variant—a wyvern-class one."

Leonis's eyes narrowed at the word *wyvern*. True, the shape of its wings was reminiscent of the winged dragonkin he knew, but it was dotted with lumps of mineral, and its ugly, inflated body was a far cry from the wyverns Leonis knew. Those were far more graceful magical beasts than this.

"...Leo, run!"

Selia fired three shots toward the Void, but they didn't even seem to faze it.

Guess I should just destroy it... Leonis gave a small shrug.

It would mean showing the girl a glimpse of his powers, but there was no helping that. On the other hand, this Void was the perfect opponent for some post-reincarnation practice.

I will make you rue the day you dared to intrude upon the Undead King Leonis's mausoleum.

An indomitable smile played over Leonis's lips as he began

weaving an ancient spell. He could feel the mana running throughout his body. This body wasn't quite at its prime, of course, but...

Shaaaaaaaaaaaaaaaaaaaaaaaaa!

The massive Void swung its talons down.

I'll turn you to dust.

Leonis began chanting a sixth-order attack spell, but then...

"...I won't let you!"

Riselia jumped in front of the boy, knocking him away.

...Huh?

Riselia's silvery hair filled Leonis's field of vision. The Void's talons descended, gouging into Riselia's upper half.

Riiiiiiiiiiiip!

The horizontal sweep knocked Riselia back. Her body bounced and rolled a few times as it crashed into the ground.

"What...?!"

Leonis got to his feet and turned to face her.

"Aaah, kh... Ugh..."

Blood quickly stained Riselia's clothes red as she lay collapsed. Leonis's eyes widened as he stood stock-still.

"Why...?"

"...R-run..." Riselia's lips parted as she feebly muttered. "Regroup with...Regina...and run... You can do that, right...?"

Her voice was all too kind but desperate. With each breath, the wound on her chest widened and blood flowed freely, coloring the earth. Leonis sensed other Voids moving behind them. The one called a wyvern class wasn't alone, it seemed. Likely two or three more of them of at least the same size appeared. Leonis, however, did not turn to face them.

"...H-h-hurry...!"

"..."

Leonis took the young woman's hand as her consciousness faded. Her fingers rapidly grew colder. He was familiar with the sensation of death. He'd come into contact with it many times already.

Calling it a foolish act of self-sacrifice would be easy. The Undead King would've never been struck by an attack like that. This was just some human girl Leonis had kept alive out of a need for information and on something of a whim. She had saved his life once—but to Leonis, she was nothing more or less than that.

But seeing Riselia rise up to protect him reminded the reincarnated Dark Lord of the way *she* had looked back then.

—*Do you see how tedious and dull being a hero really is? Become mine instead, Leonis.*

Riselia reminded him of a girl who had risked life and limb to protect an injured boy. The girl who had appeared before him when he was betrayed by the ones he'd saved... Riselia reminded him of the Goddess of Rebellion. The one who raised the banner of discord, the one despised by the rest of the world.

"...It really is all too incorrigible," Leonis whispered bitterly as he dipped his fingers into the puddle of blood.

"This body...is completely and utterly incorrigible..."

Why did a return to a human body mean the return of human emotions...?

Leonis rose to his feet and glanced back. At the moment, the three Voids seemed frozen in place, evidently taken aback by the overwhelming presence coming from the boy. He looked around, taking in the destruction spotting the walls of the ruin.

"You cretins dared disturb my resting place," the child said coldly. "I'd thought I'd been reincarnated, only to find myself in this worthless shell. Strange monsters now run amok in my mausoleum as if they own the place. And now they've slain the girl who saved my life. Yes, that's right, I admit it. This courageous girl managed to earn some of my interest..."

Leonis ignored the Voids, continuing to mutter to himself.

"And this robe is too large to move in comfortably, and honestly, my feet hurt..."

He'd had to run across the stone floor with bare feet, cutting and scraping them all the while.

That last one was mostly just his griping, but still...

"—Now, then. I suppose I should grant you fools a fitting punishment." Leonis crossed his arms, pondering.

The Undead King was a tolerant sort and willing to take extenuating circumstances into account. What was he to do? These creatures seemingly lacked intelligence, after all. They lacked the capacity to understand what they were doing and who they were dealing with.

They never suspected that this seemingly frail boy was one they should have never, ever sought as an enemy.

"Well, I suppose that in the end..." The Undead King turned a quick glance at Riselia's bloodied body before passing judgment.

"You fools deserve nothing but certain death."

Leonis stomped his feet atop his shadow beneath him. The shadow writhed eerily, and from within it rose a single staff. A blue magic crystal was embedded in the tip of the rod.

"It's been around a thousand years, my faithful companion."

At Leonis's slightest touch, the staff loosed a tremendously ominous aura.

The symbol of death of the Dark Lords' Armies—the Staff of Sealed Sins. It was the demon eye staff Leonis had stolen during a battle against a divine dragon.

"Hmm. It's a bit too long for this body, isn't it?"

Holding the staff with one hand, Leonis examined it closely, when...

Shaaaaaaaaaaaaaaaaaaaaaaaaaaaaaaaaaaaaaaaaaaaaaaa!

The wyvern-class Void swooped down with its talons again.

"—My word. How uncouth."

Leonis charged the staff with mana and fired off a spell.

Crack...

The Void's massive form was assailed by a powerful pressure and crushed from above. Its four limbs bent and contorted in unnatural directions, and its head was pushed down against the ground so hard, it left an impression.

The magic was an eighth-order gravity-type spell, the Grand Pressure Wave, Vira Zuo. The Void's appendages twitched desperately from within the increased gravity, but the creature was unable to stand.

"I will grind you into the soil, you inferior existence."

With a tap of the tip of the staff to the ground...

The Void disintegrated, its cry of death distorted by the gravity well.

Rooooooooooaaar!

A horned, beast-like Void charged Leonis.

"So you are incapable of knowing fear. How amusing."

Leonis stuck out his staff.

"Rua Meires."

The staff's eye shone, and a gleaming hexagonal barrier sprouted in front of Leonis. The beast-like Void's charge was easily brought to a halt by the magical construct.

"What? Is this the best you can do?" Leonis gave a thin smile.

The tip of the Void's horns made contact with the barrier, releasing powerful bolts of electricity in an attempt to break through the Undead King's defense. The attack failed to penetrate the magical shield, though.

"Well then, allow me to take the next step."

Leonis swung his staff downwards. The hexagonal barrier began spinning rapidly, easily shredding the animallike Void.

The remaining Void was reminiscent of a serpent and seemed to possess a bit more intelligence than the other two. It burrowed into the walls of the ruin, trying to flee to a lower level.

"Do you really think I'd let you escape?"

Leonis kicked against the ground and levitated into the air. He swung his staff toward the Void burrowing its way down.

"I will burn you to cinders!"

He cast an eighth-order fire-type spell, the Grand Annihilation Fireball, Al Gu Belzelga.

Kabooooooooooooooooooooooom!

Crimson flames scorched the Void to ash in a matter of seconds.

"...Well, that was simple enough," Leonis muttered as he landed gently on the ground. However, his expression quickly turned to shock.

"I-impossible!"

There was something there that should not have been. It seemed the charred skeletal remains of the snakelike Void remained.

"How could its bones endure after taking a hit from an Al Gu Belzelga spell?!"

Those were intense flames summoned directly from the Realm of Muspelheim, capable of melting even the scales of a red dragon.

Looking down at his hands, Leonis sighed in disappointment. Back when he was still known as a hero, magic had actually been a weakness of his. It seemed this form simply didn't have the same magical abilities he'd had in his prime.

...A third of that, at best, from the look of things.

Leonis approached Riselia and took her hands in his. Her skin was growing colder, but she still drew faint breath. The human body is a frail thing, though. She'd surely die at this rate. Her pale face was gruesome to the point of beauty.

"I am a Dark Lord. The lives of humans mean nothing to me." Leonis made sure to whisper the words, even though she likely couldn't hear him.

"But I do respect your noble soul. You risked your life to protect me. Trying to defend a Dark Lord is impudent to the point of blasphemy, but I will acknowledge your spirit." Leonis wrapped his arms around her bloodstained body.

"Kh... You're heavy, aren't you...?"

She was actually quite dainty for a girl her age, but for Leonis's newly reborn ten-year-old frame, it was quite the weight.

"My apologies, but while I've devoted myself to sorcery, holy magic is the one thing I cannot use."

That was the price those who dabbled in the Realm of Death's magic had to pay. The Undead King Leonis could not use even the most basic or rudimentary healing spells, to say nothing of restoring someone who had lost so much of their life force.

As such...

Leonis elected to save her using the only other method he knew.

CHAPTER 2

THE WORLD. ONE THOUSAND YEARS LATER

How many times had she seen this dream?

A burning city, the screams of fleeing people, monsters filling the sky. Six years ago, Riselia Crystalia's family was slain by the Voids.

The commanding Void Lord went on a large-scale Stampede, attacking the Third Assault Garden, which happened to be near the city where her parents and older sister served as governors and Holy Swordsmen, commanding the knights. They'd gone to the front lines to halt the advance of the Voids and to protect the people. They'd all died in battle.

Riselia was nine years old at the time, and only she and her childhood friend Regina managed to evacuate to the shelter and survive.

Those days were truly hellish. But soon after, the two of them were secured by a search party dispatched by the Seventh Assault Garden that was looking for survivors. They were sent to Excalibur Academy to train as Holy Swordswomen.

Holy Swords—a power granted to humanity by the planet and

the only one capable of opposing the Voids. They often took the forms of weapons, granting their wielders various abilities.

Riselia spent her days at Excalibur Academy training herself to the bone, hoping to develop the strength to use a Holy Sword and fight the Voids as a Holy Swordswoman... But even after all her efforts, her Holy Sword had never manifested...

What was worse...

I'm going to die here...aren't I...?

The cold, creeping feeling of death washed over her body. As her consciousness faded, her thoughts wandered to the boy again. Was he able to meet up with Regina and escape? No... Even if she had bought him a few more seconds of life, he likely wouldn't have been able to get away.

...I'm sorry...I couldn't...protect you...

The girl's thoughts faded into blackness...

◆

"...No good. I don't understand this thing at all."

Frustrated, Leonis tossed the card-type terminal he'd found on Riselia into the rubble of the caved-in ruin. It seemed to contain a kind of magic circuitry, but even Leonis's knowledge of the arcane didn't allow him to make sense of how it worked.

"I never imagined mankind's magic technology would develop this far."

...That much, at least, he could understand. Things were more developed than they'd been a thousand years ago, at least as far as magical technology went.

What I really can't wrap my mind around is that weapon they called a Holy Sword.

The girl named Regina had used it to fire an attack of breathtaking power. And the energy fueling it seemed to stem from principles that differed entirely from the magic Leonis knew.

Perhaps the weapon was unique in some way, or...?

The Dark Lord let out a sigh. The monsters that attacked the ruins, the Voids. Those didn't exist one thousand years ago. Neither did this highly advanced magical technology or the Holy Swords. Would he really be able to find *her* in this world...?

—The Goddess of Rebellion's prophecy: One thousand years into the future, the power of the reincarnated goddess will be reborn.

Leonis's mission was to find the vessel into which she would reincarnate and then defend her until the time of her awakening. After that, he was to rebuild the Dark Lords' Armies that once stood against the gods.

That was the sole promise Leonis, the Undead King, had ever given her.

"...Mmm, ugh, aah... Mm..."

Riselia's brow furrowed gently as she lay at Leonis's side.

...She's waking up.

Leonis's spell proved fruitful, successfully resuscitating the girl even as she was on the verge of death. Although the end result far exceeded Leonis's expectations...

...He'd never imagined things would go as well as they had.

How unusual. Perhaps she is uniquely compatible?

He turned his gaze to Riselia, who was rubbing her eyes sleepily... The symptoms would likely surface later. She would probably grow angry when she learned the truth.

She may very well fall into despair..., Leonis thought, all the while wishing she wouldn't come to hate him for it.

Riselia, however, took no notice of the child's inner conflict...

"...Huh...? Huh? Huuuuh?!" She looked down at her body and exclaimed with shock.

"Good morning, Miss Selia," Leonis said.

"Ah..." Riselia's mouth and her ice-blue eyes were all wide with surprise, but after a few moments of stupefied silence...she snared Leonis in a hug.

"...Wait, what?!"

"...Thank goodness... You're safe...," she said softly in relief.

...I'd think she'd be more worried about herself.

Leonis sighed as she embraced him.

"Erm, it's getting a bit difficult to breathe..."

"Oh, sorry... Wait, how am I...?"

Riselia let go of him and looked down at her chest. Her uniform had been torn by the Void's talons and stained with blood. The fabric still bore horizontal cuts, but the wounds on her flesh had completely closed.

"...I can't believe it... I thought I was dead for sure..."

"The injuries weren't as bad as they seemed," Leonis lied nonchalantly. "Because of that, I was able to heal you with holy sorcery."

"Source-sery...?" Riselia gave a quizzical look, peering at Leonis's face intently.

"Erm..." Leonis was taken aback by her unexpected response.

And after a moment of thought...

It dawned on him. ...*Could it be she doesn't know what sorcery is?*

Now that Leonis thought about it, he hadn't seen anyone use sorcery during the battle with the Voids earlier. But Riselia did use some kind of tool made with advanced magic circuits. What did it all mean?

...No, that's not it. Perhaps I've got it backward.

They couldn't use sorcery, so they used special equipment with magic circuits that anyone could use without any training. All one would need was a bit of mana.

Shoot...

Leonis tried to find the words to smooth things over, but then...

"Do you mean the power of a Holy Sword?"

"...Um, yes, I suppose?" Leonis decided to go with it.

"I see. Excalibur Academy has confirmed the existence of Holy Swords with healing powers." Riselia nodded. "So you're a Holy Sword wielder. That might actually explain why the Voids abducted you...," she muttered to herself, resting her chin on her hand.

"...Uh, I actually don't really know much about how this power works. What are Holy Swords, exactly?" Leonis asked, deciding now would be a good time to inquire.

The term *Holy Sword* in this era likely meant something quite different from the holy swords the Undead King knew from his own time.

"Right, that makes sense. People from outside the Assault Gardens probably wouldn't know."

"Yes." Leonis nodded.

"Holy Swords are a power mankind awakened to in order to fight the Voids."

Riselia explained that sixty-four years ago, mankind came under attack by the Voids—distorted invaders from another world. Three-fourths of mankind was lost in the tragedy. A few years later, as despair was closing in, people discovered that some children had begun exhibiting unique powers.

"The children were given miraculous gifts. They could manipulate fire, control the movements of the winds, and many other abilities, all capable of defeating the Voids. Most of them took the form of weapons, so they came to be known as Holy Swords."

"...So the weapon that blond lady used earlier was a Holy Sword, too?"

"Yes, that was her Holy Sword, Drag Howl. A manifestation of destructive power. The exact reason isn't understood, but apparently, Holy Swords often reflect the personalities of their wielders."

...A weapon that's a manifestation of one's soul. I see.

It was a bit hard to immediately believe, but if true, this was a power of a different category altogether from the death magic Leonis used...and from holy and spirit magics as well.

"Children who awaken to the power of a Holy Sword are sent to the Holy Swordsmen training institute—also known as Excalibur Academy—to hone and master their power."

Leonis inferred that meant Riselia held the power of a Holy Sword, too. She hadn't used it earlier, though...

...Regardless, that would mean the sorcery I use only exists as a faded legend in this age.

Yet another piece of new information regarding this world.

I should probably hide that I can use it...

Riselia brushed her fingers over the wounds on her chest.

"A Holy Sword with the power of healing... You must have a very kind heart, Leo."

"........."

Riselia beamed, and Leonis couldn't help but look away.

...What kind of expression would she make upon learning the truth?

"You saved my life."

"No, Miss Selia, if you hadn't protected me, that creature would've killed me..."

At his words, Riselia gasped and looked around as if remembering something.

"Th-that's right, where did that Void go?"

"I, um, got scared and closed my eyes, but at some point, it just disappeared." Leonis shook his head.

...Technically, it wasn't a lie.

Leonis had stored the remains of the three Voids by having his shadow swallow them whole.

"...It disappeared?"

"Yes."

"I see. The Voids do have a way of doing the incomprehensible...," Riselia mused, placing a hand over her beautiful chin.

"Erm, just what are the Voids?" Leonis asked for the second time.

"...Honestly, we don't really know." She shook her head silently. "They're a threat to mankind that appeared sixty-four years ago. They're a completely unknown enemy. Their goals, where they might appear: It's all a mystery. Them being invaders from another world is just one of the administration bureau's theories. No one really knows. That's why we call them Voids—they're emptiness."

Leonis couldn't help but wonder what was going on. Was the world really infested with completely unknown monsters?

"You said some things earlier. 'Ogre' and 'wyvern'..."

"Those are general classes of Voids. They're named, based on their appearances, after legendary monsters that existed back in ancient times."

"Legendary..." The word stuck in the back of Leonis's throat.

So did the monsters that existed one thousand years ago exist no longer...?

Riselia rose to her feet.

"It might come back. We should hurry and get out of here."

"...Right."

Riselia touched one of her earrings.

"Regina, do you read?"

"Lady Selia, are you all right?!" The girl's relieved voice echoed. **"I was worried when I lost contact with you. Where are you now?"**

"Still inside the ruins. What about that ogre class?"

"It took eight shots from the Drag Cannon but finally went down. Bulky bastard."

"Roger... We'll regroup at the entrance."

With that, Riselia cut off the transmission.

"We shouldn't dawdle in a place like this. Let's go."

...A place like this? Leonis thought, indignant.

◆

"There's the exit, Leo."

"*Haff, haff...* Yes."

A few hours of climbing up the ruin's stratums later, the two finally reached the exit to the surface.

Ugh... I have to confess, I may have dug the mausoleum too deep...

Leonis couldn't help but regret his former actions as he dragged his wobbling legs. Climbing seven levels was taxing on his ten-year-old body. He could have taken himself and his companion out straightaway using the teleportation circle, but explaining to Riselia how he knew about such a thing felt like it was more trouble than it was worth.

"You really gave it your all," Riselia said, walking ahead of him. She reached out a hand to help the panting boy. Wordlessly, he extended his own as well, and she pulled him up.

...My dignity as the Undead King is tarnished.

They had exited a cave that led into the underground of the Ruin Mountains. A sandy gust of wind blew at them. Beyond the entrance to the ruins lay a vast wasteland. The sun was out but hidden behind a curtain of gray clouds, casting a gloomy dimness over the area.

...The ruins of Necrozoa are probably right beneath our feet.

The capital of the dead, which had flourished and prospered

one thousand years ago, now lay buried without a trace beneath the sand. Even if it were to be excavated, it'd likely be nothing more than a dilapidated husk...

"Lady Selia—" The calm voice of a girl caught their ears.

Turning, the two saw a blond with pigtails, wearing a hood to shield her face from the sand. She was straddling a lump of metal that was likely some kind of vehicle. It was the girl who'd used that cannon earlier, Regina.

"I'm glad to see you're fine... Wait, what's with all this blood?!"

"Erm, well, aah..." Riselia nodded awkwardly. "We couldn't find the hive, but we did confirm the appearance of several more Voids. We should report it to the academy's administration bureau."

"Several more? You fought off multiple Voids?!" Regina said, surprised.

"Yes, but they seem to have just disappeared."

"...Huh."

Regina turned her attention to Leonis, who stood behind Riselia.

"...And who's the kid?"

"A refugee child I discovered and took under my protection in the ruin. Voids abducted him, and from the looks of it, his memories have been mixed up."

"Voids took a child?"

"We can't deny the possibility. There's still a lot we don't know about Void biology. If he can reclaim his memories, his testimony could be a source of valuable information."

Regina nodded in agreement. "I wonder if there's a refugee village nearby."

"Who's to say? We haven't investigated this area at all, and for all we know, he could've been carried here from far off by a flying-type Void."

Regina squatted next to Leonis, meeting his gaze at eye level. Her large chest bouncing as she did so.

"...?!"

"I'm Lady Selia's maid, Regina Mercedes. It's nice to meet you."

"Y-yes, nice to meet you..."

...Leonis nodded, overwhelmed by the sight of her breasts bobbing in front of his eyes.

"Lady Selia, this boy is surprisingly pervy," Regina whispered into Riselia's ear.

"...Wh—?!"

"Geez. What do you think you're saying?!"

Ignoring her maid's nonsense, Riselia straddled the odd vehicle. It had three wheels and was reminiscent of a small carriage, but there were no horses in sight.

"What is this?"

"A military vehicle. Take a seat behind me, Leo."

Riselia leaned forward, and Leonis wrapped his arms around her waist. The soft texture made his heart skip a beat.

"This thing can really fly, so hang on tight."

Regina hopped onto the side seat.

"Feel free to enjoy the sensation of Lady Selia's body to the fullest until we reach town, kid."

"Stop that, Regina!" Riselia scolded as she kicked the pedal.

"Whoaaaaaa!"

The vehicle immediately took off at high speed.

◆

The military transport kicked up a cloud of dust as it zoomed across the wasteland at a breathtaking pace.

...I-it goes this fast?! Leonis's expression was strained as he clutched Riselia's waist tightly.

Honestly speaking, it was far from a comfortable ride. A world of difference from the black wolf he'd once ridden into battle. Riselia's silver hair trailed behind her, brushing Leonis's face gently. The scent of her sweat filled his nostrils as he clung to her.

"I think I'll hit the showers as soon as I return to the academy."

"Yeah. Even my underwear's full of sand." Regina, who was sitting in the sidecar, tugged down the collar of her uniform toward her chest.

"...Hey there, kid, whatcha looking at?"

"I-I'm not looking at anything!" Leonis hurriedly buried his face in Riselia's back.

"Hmm, reaaaaaally?" A teasing smile moved across Regina's lips.

This lass dares treat the Undead King like this...!

Riselia held her ear down with one hand and began transmitting a report to someone.

"I've rescued a refugee child. We're returning to the academy right now."

"Roger that. I'll have the gate open and submit an application to the bureau."

"I know I'm your junior, but could you please prepare a uniform set, too?"

"A uniform?"

"Yes, I've already sent the size data for you."

"...Understood. I'll have it prepared."

"...Um. There's something I've been wanting to ask," Leonis said to Regina.

"What is it, kid?"

"What exactly is a refugee?"

Regina's face turned serious.

"Sixty-four years ago, the people of various countries who were attacked by Voids gathered in colonies that started popping up. That was before the empire began the Assault Garden project. People who had to flee their home nations are called refugees. The purposes of the Assault Gardens are to discover and stomp out the source of Voids and also to seek out and gather missing refugees."

"Are there are a lot of refugees out there?"

"Even the Garden's administration bureau doesn't have a handle on the exact number. The Void invasion completely changed the world, after all."

"...I see."

"You really did lose your memories, huh?"

"...Erm, I'm sorry." Leonis spoke with a flustered tone, worrying Regina might be suspicious.

"Don't be. I'm the one who should be apologizing. I'm sorry."

"........."

Regina gave the boy a meek sort of look.

...Perhaps she'd only teased him to help loosen him up a bit.

"Heh-heh, maybe a little shock will jog your memories?"

The girl flipped up her skirt, granting Leonis a glimpse of her thighs.

"...Th-that's okay, I'm fine!"

...She wasn't trying to help him at all. Regina was just taunting him for fun!

"Regina, what are you doing?!" Riselia demanded, having now finished her transmission.

"Why, absolutely nothing at all, Lady Selia."

"What'll you do if Leo becomes a perverted kid?!"

"If I may make an observation, Lady Selia, all boys already are pervs." Regina shrugged.

...Leonis shook his head in adamant denial. The Undead King Leonis had nothing to do with this. The only reason his eyes wandered in that direction was due to a physiological reaction stemming from his adolescent body.

The vehicle continued running across the wasteland, until...

The gray clouds gave way to a vast blue sky.

"You can almost see it in the distance."

"...?!"

He shielded his eyes from the dazzling sunlight. It was a light he hadn't bathed in since becoming the Undead King. Trees dotted the landscape; vast plains spread out in all directions. And farther beyond...

He could see the ocean.

And...

"...Wh-what in the world?!" Leonis cried out in his natural voice despite himself.

A massive city sat on the ocean, illuminated by sunlight.

"This is a final bastion of mankind, built to oppose Voids. It's one of the eight great city-states built around the capital of Camelot. It's a castle for countless Holy Swordsmen and the instrument of our counterattack," Riselia declared proudly.

"The Seventh Assault Garden."

CHAPTER 3

THE SEVENTH ASSAULT GARDEN

The vehicle ran over a massive bridge that crossed the sea. Wind rich with the scent of salt fluttered through Riselia's silvery hair.

...The land of darkness, huh?

This place was once a part of the plains. It'd been the site of the final battle of the Dark Lords' Armies. One thousand years ago, Archsage Arakael of the Six Heroes fused with the Holy Tree and consumed the forces of the Dark Lords in a sea of trees...

Trees that now slumbered at the bottom of this ocean.

Whatever happened in the last thousand years, it had changed the terrain greatly.

...The whole area looks like it's been transformed into a gulf. I suppose it connected with an ocean at some point.

Still clinging to Riselia's body, Leonis turned his gaze to the island towering ahead.

Yes, it was an island.

An extraordinarily massive island surrounded by ramparts. The walls were outfitted with innumerable gun ports staring down at them.

It's even larger than Rivaiz's sea fortress..., Leonis thought.

Rivaiz, the Lord of the Seas, once reigned over the seven demonic oceans. He met his demise in mutual defeat against the mage Diruda, another of the Six Heroes. Both of them had been sent somewhere beyond this dimension.

"Is this your first time seeing an Assault Garden, Leo?"

"Ah, yes... It's amazing. It's hard to believe they could build such a large artificial island."

"Right... How can you tell it's artificial, though?"

"Ah, well..."

That was because there weren't any islands here a thousand years ago, so he naturally concluded it must be artificial.

"It's surrounded by castle walls, and there's no natural rock coming up from the water."

"The Assault Garden's a manmade mega-float. All the electricity and food the city uses are produced internally," Regina explained. "The city's standing here right now, but it can move across the sea. Assault Gardens exist to strike down Void colonies, after all."

"This island can move...?" Leonis swallowed, hard.

The Dark Lords' Armies had a mobile stronghold called the Blue Sky Citadel, but it wasn't anything like this place in terms of scale. If what Regina said was to be believed, then mankind had achieved an unprecedented level of cultural advancement.

...And there are seven cities of this size?

Humans.

They were no match for the demi-human races in terms of strength and weren't as civilized as the elves. But now they had achieved such an impressive civilization...

...It would be wise to analyze mankind's current strength in the name of the resurgence of the Dark Lords' Armies.

Their vehicle was soon admitted through the Assault Garden's front gate.

◆

"Some humans granted the power of Holy Swords. Those who possess it are required to be admitted into Excalibur Academy. Fighting the Voids isn't compulsory, but one is still required to help out in some way," Riselia explained as she got off the vehicle.

"...I see."

Admission into this academy would actually be beneficial. Rationally speaking, it would allow him to learn more about the Holy Swords.

"All right, we'll meet up again later. If you get lost—," Riselia said with concern in her voice.

"Lady Selia, it's a straight walk forward. He'll be fine." Regina cut her off with a hint of exasperation.

Apparently, people brought in from the outside had to go through a special inspection of some sort. Leonis stood at the start of a corridor lit by a mana flare. A metallic partition closed behind him when he separated from the two girls. As soon as he was alone, Leonis let out a long breath and shouted:

"How in the world did things come to this?!"

According to his flawless, infallible plan, he was supposed to awaken from his thousand-year slumber to the cheers of his reverent worshippers and rebuild the Dark Lords' Armies to strike the time-weakened forces of mankind.

Instead, humanity was overwhelmingly advanced, and the sorcery of old had declined. What's more, it wasn't the magical races of the ages but some unidentified specters called Voids running amok in the world.

...And on top of everything, I look like this.

Why had his spell of reincarnation failed...?

Leonis had one theory. A thousand years ago, Leonis had woven the spell so as to revive in his Undead King body. However, before he became the Undead King, he had been a human hero. He was betrayed by mankind and was on the cusp of dying when the Goddess of Rebellion saved him.

In other words, I had two past lives. One as a hero, and one as the Undead King.

As such, his plan was to reincarnate in two phases. First, he would be reborn in his original body, his hero one. He would then rebuild the Undead King body granted to him by the goddess. But for whatever reason, that attempt had failed. He'd awakened before his Undead King body had been re-formed.

But whatever the case...

...It will take me time to get accustomed to this body. He moaned bitterly as he held up the empty hems of his robe.

Still, there's no need to be pessimistic.

Meeting Riselia Crystalia and coming here was a stroke of luck, and being in this city gave him an effective means of gathering intelligence.

Leonis looked down at his shadow.

"—Blackas, Shary," he called.

Sss. Sssss. Ssssssssss.

His shadow began twisting about as something as dark as obsidian crawled out of it. The first to emerge was a black wolf with golden eyes. His body was twice as large and thick as an ordinary wolf, and his fur was darker than the blackest night.

The second shadow took a humanoid form: a girl with dignified, dimly lit eyes, clad in a trim and proper maid's uniform. She looked to be about twelve or thirteen years old. Her raven hair, cut evenly around her shoulders, had a sleek luster to it.

"—Did you call for me, my friend?"

"Did you summon me, my lord?"

The black wolf addressed Leonis as one would a peer, while the girl kneeled reverently before him.

"It has been a long time, you two," Leonis replied, giving a well-practiced wave of the hand.

The black wolf was a brother in arms, who had once run across the fields of battle with him, and prince of the Realm of Shadows.

The girl was once an assassin of the Realm of Shadows who had tried to claim Leonis's life. After a certain series of events, she'd become a maid in service to the Undead King.

When the Six Heroes ravaged the Realm of Shadows, Leonis had allowed a portion of it to take refuge in his shadow. These two were its survivors.

...There was actually one other kept in his shadow, but if they were to see Leonis as he was now, they'd gleefully try to kill him in his sleep.

"Aye. That millennium of slumber did feel rather long," replied the black wolf, Blackas Shadow Prince.

None among the Undead King's followers would speak to him in such an insolent, casual manner. However, Blackas wasn't a follower but rather a friend and equal to Leonis.

"More to the point, how did you end up in that form?"

"A minor misjudgment. I've been reincarnated into the body I once had as a human," Leonis said with awkward vagueness.

"The Hero of the Holy Sword, hmm? I believe this is the first time I've seen you like this."

"By the time we'd met, I was already the Undead King."

"My lord."

"What is it, Shary?" Leonis looked back at the girl, who eyed him shyly.

"I find your current appearance exceptionally cute, my lord."

"Are you making light of me, Shary?"

"...Perish the thought, my lord," Shary apologized in a flustered manner. Her lord, his eyes half-lidded, gave a shake of his head.

"...No matter. I've summoned you two because I must ask something of you both."

"Order me as you will, my lord." The girl bowed her head.

"I will gladly lend you my strength, my friend." The black wolf nodded.

"I want you to investigate this city. This world is far too different from what I imagined before my return."

Blackas gave a grunt of consent, looking around curiously.

"Things truly have changed beyond all recognition while we slumbered," he agreed.

"They have. Sorcery has declined over the years, so using it would attract unwanted attention."

Compensating for the loss of sorcery, mankind had created a civilization around artifacts that could activate magic instead. The lighting illuminating the corridor would have been considered a precious magic tool one thousand years ago.

"But if sorcery has declined, how could they create things like these without any knowledge of it?"

"That's something else we need to look into. At any rate, I can't use my magic publicly, so I'll have to rely on you two."

"Understood."

"By your will, my lord."

The two disappeared back into his shadow. Leaving the

investigation of the city to them, Leonis could focus his efforts on Excalibur Academy.

The boy stepped down the corridor. Suddenly, a shrill alarm began to blare. A mana detector was going off.

"What?!" Leonis quickly chanted a magic obfuscation spell. The spell took hold, and the alarm stopped.

...I'll need to be cautious.

◆

The examination took fifteen minutes or so and was completely unmanned. Upon completing it, Leonis boarded an elevator. When the door opened, he stepped outside into blinding sunlight and found Riselia waiting for him.

"Good job, Leo," she said, handing him a card. "This is your ID card. Well, a temporary one, at least."

"Card?" Leonis eyed the blue tile curiously.

At its center was an icon with the simple design of a white sword. He didn't need to use a mana detection spell to tell some kind of magic was embedded in it.

"This is proof of your identity in the Assault Garden. Make sure you don't lose it, okay?"

"All right."

"Then let's head to the academy," Riselia said, tapping the vehicle's seat, which was still dirty with sand.

Leonis looked at the conveyance with confusion, noticing the sidecar was gone.

"Where's Regina?"

"She said needed to do some shopping, so she's off in the commercial district."

"I see."

Apparently, the sidecar could become a transport vehicle of its own. Leonis sat down on the seat like before and wrapped his arms around Riselia's waist. The engine rumbled as she pushed down on the pedal, and the vehicle sped down the tunnel.

The ground was paved, so it was a much smoother ride compared to when they'd been driving across the wasteland. The wind was pleasant, and Riselia's silver hair trailed behind her as they cruised along. And when they left the tunnel...

"Wha...?!" Leonis's mouth fell open in surprise.

Before the two stood an enormous laminated structure.

"This is the commercial district," Riselia explained. "Impressive, isn't it?"

"Erm, yes, I suppose," the boy replied with false composure.

"Everyone's surprised the first time they see it." The silver-haired girl was apparently disappointed by Leonis's response.

The high-rise was dotted with countless windows. Leonis had never seen anything like it. The technology needed to create such a multistoried building could never have existed in his native era.

Many other boys and girls were walking about, all sporting the same uniform. Clearly, they were Riselia's fellow students at Excalibur Academy.

"It feels surprisingly peaceful here."

"You can tell?"

"That's the kind of atmosphere this place gives off..."

He was well acquainted with what a country in wartime looked like and found it hard to believe this place was at the front line of the battle against Voids.

"The Seventh Assault Garden has never allowed a Void to penetrate its walls," Riselia explained. "It's the newest city, if you don't count the Eighth Assault Garden. That one's still under construction.

Holy Swordsmen are dispatched to fight on the front lines, but the city itself is safe."

"I see."

"The Garden is divided into a residential and a commercial district, and in the center is the administration bureau, which unifies the whole city. And the part that governs military affairs..." The young woman raised a finger, pointing ahead.

"...is Excalibur Academy, the core of the city."

◆

"Before we register you for the Academy, you should probably take a bath."

Going through the gate, Riselia parked the vehicle in an open parking space within the academy grounds. Excalibur Academy's premises were vast and comprised of several combined facilities.

...How is this possible? This place is far larger than even a Dark Lord's castle. Upon disembarking, Leonis was overwhelmed by the sheer scale of the academy.

"Are these all academy facilities?"

"Yes. It's all a bit stunning at first." Riselia gave a nod before explaining.

"That's the great auditorium," she started. "That building over there is where the cafeterias are. There are restaurants in the city's commercial district, but the cafeterias are affordable, and their meals are really tasty." Leonis's tour continued. "The area sitting right in the middle of the academy is the outdoor training ground. Students train using a personalized regimen built to match the unique abilities of their Holy Swords. Lastly, there's the library, the laboratories, a dance hall, leisure facilities, and a sauna next to the dorms."

"Erm, I understand what the training ground is for, but why do you need a dance hall and a sauna?" Leonis wondered aloud.

"Holy Swords are weapons born of one's heart. Neglecting the needs of your heart inhibits your ability to wield that power. Actually, the Second Assault Garden had more standard training facilities, but the results weren't all that satisfactory."

"...I see."

So this place employed more unorthodox training methodologies.

The two continued to walk, heading down a boulevard of broad-leaved trees. They passed a group of girls in the same kind of navy-blue uniform that Riselia wore. The girls took one look at Leonis and promptly assailed him with all manner of comments unsuitable for the Undead King, like: "Look at him, he's so cute!"

"Are girls more common at this academy?"

"The gender ratio is about fifty-fifty, but this sector has the girls' dorms—" Riselia cut herself off.

"...?"

Leonis looked up at the silver-haired girl. Her expression was tense, her lips pursed. Standing a few dozen paces ahead was a blond boy in an academy uniform.

"Well, if it's isn't Miss Riselia. Hello, there. What brings you here?"

"Muselle Rhodes..." Riselia took a cautious step back.

...He doesn't look like a friend of hers.

The young man named Muselle was tailed by a group of four academy girls, all beautiful... Though, of course, none were a match for the beauty of the girl standing at Leonis's side.

Muselle himself had a handsome face, though his vulgar expression hardly matched. He gave off a rude sort of air as he looked Riselia up and down, evaluating her.

...There was something about it that was off-putting.

"Let's go, Leo." Riselia tugged at the boy's arm to lead him away.

"Hmm? And where would you be off to?" Muselle and the girls waiting on him blocked Riselia's exit, their shoes squeaking slightly as they moved.

"...Please step aside," requested Riselia.

"Come now, no need to be so cold... Hmm, who's this kid?" The young man looked down, obviously noticing Leonis for the first time.

"You might be my senior, but who he is has nothing to do with you." Riselia glared at him, resolute. Her adversary suppressed a laugh.

"My, if this isn't fantastic! The dropout squad is bringing in a child now!"

"...Kh. He's a full-fledged Holy Swordsman."

"This boy? Ah-ha-ha, spare me the jokes!" Muselle's voice was bold as he looked down at Leonis with a sneer.

...*Good grief. Ignorance truly is bliss, isn't it...?* The Undead King shrugged mentally.

In any other situation, he'd have reduced this boy to ash a hundred times over and reanimated him as a skeleton warrior, the lowest of undead servants. Had Shary been here, this brat would be a smear on the ground by now.

...*But I suppose I can't fault anyone for doubting my abilities because of how I appear right now. I'll look past his attitude, if only so as not to make myself conspicuous...*

Noticing Leonis wasn't stirred by his provocation, Muselle returned his attention to Riselia. "You should stop trying so hard and just join my platoon already, Riselia Crystalia. If you join the highest-ranking platoon, perhaps you'll be allowed to remain in the academy." Muselle's lips twisted into a grin, and he spoke as if to make sure Leonis heard him. "Even if you *can't manifest a Holy Sword despite being the daughter of such distinguished Holy Swordsmen.*"

"...!"

Riselia glared at Muselle through narrowed eyes.

She doesn't have a Holy Sword? Leonis thought suspiciously. *Come to think of it, she didn't use one back in the ruin.*

No... It wasn't that she didn't. She couldn't.

That was why she had to jump in and use her body to protect Leonis from the Void's talons. But if that was the case, why was she enrolled in an academy for training Holy Swordsmen...?

"You don't have to throw yourself into dangerous Void investigations. You need only join my collection of toys."

Muselle's smile took on a vulgar, perverted sheen as he reached for one of the girls standing beside him and began fondling her breasts. The girl only shivered in faint reaction but showed no resistance, as if she were a doll lacking its own will. She simply let Muselle grope her to his heart's content.

What is that? Some kind of enslavement or mental manipulation spell? No...

The sorcery of a millennia ago had been lost to the ages. In which case...

It must be a Holy Sword...

...Leonis understood. Holy Swords could be more than the cannon-type that Regina had. The Undead King would have to adjust his perception of what a Holy Sword could be.

"...I refuse," Riselia answered flatly.

Muselle clicked his tongue in annoyance.

"You dare ignore the goodwill I show you?!" he shouted. Clearly irritated, he pushed away the girl he was fondling.

You call this "goodwill"...? Leonis was quickly getting fed up with this.

This young man seemingly harbored some distorted desires... some warped lust for Riselia.

She's fair enough to make the Undead King stop in awe, after all.

"—Step aside." Again, Riselia tried to ignore him and walk away.

"...Tch. Wait. What's with that attitude? Do you think you're better than me?!"

"...Ow!" A pained sound came from the girl's mouth as her expression stiffened.

Muselle had grabbed her by her silvery hair.

—At that moment, the air around them grew still and cold.

"Wh-what...?" Muselle froze in place. He looked as though he'd suddenly felt the presence of death sweep over him. As if a hard hand had gripped his heart. Every pore in his body broke out in a cold sweat.

"........."

Leonis tapped at Muselle's heel with the end of his shoe. That alone was enough to make the young man fall to his knees, as if crumpling in weakness. To Riselia's eyes, it seemed he'd suddenly collapsed on the spot for no reason.

"...Ah, guh, aaah...!"

Muselle didn't have a much better idea what was going on, but he felt the creeping sense of death bearing down on him, choking his words.

"Uh, are you all right, mister?" Leonis asked with a feigned ignorance. He knelt down and took hold of Muselle's arm.

"Ahhh...!"

A sudden rush of instinctive terror made Muselle pull away, but Leonis wasn't about to let him escape. He brought his face to Muselle's ear and whispered:

"A bastard like you has no right to touch her hair. *This woman is mine.*"

He whispered each word clearly so as to be sure they were understood.

"...?!"

Leonis let go of his arm.

"Wh-what? What the hell are you...? Sh-shit!" Muselle scurried to his feet. "H-Holy Sword, Activate!" he cried with an intense expression.

"Leo...!" Riselia reflexively stepped forward to cover the boy.

But at that moment...

"Muselle Rhodes. Unauthorized use of a Holy Sword is forbidden." A dignified voice caught their ears from somewhere nearby.

Muselle clicked his tongue in annoyance and lowered his hands. Turning around, they saw the admonition had come from a girl in an academy uniform who'd been following a levitating orb. Her long black hair reached down to her waist and swayed with each of her steps. Her expression was dauntless.

"What's more, this sector is for the girls' dorms. If you do not leave at once, I will have to report you to the bureau. Are we clear?"

"Guh... I-I'll remember this!"

Muselle glared at the black-haired girl first and then cast a hateful look at Leonis before taking off with his four followers trailing after him.

...That was a bit disgraceful of me—getting this worked up over a fly like him...

Leonis knew he shouldn't be doing anything to make himself stand out here in Excalibur Academy. That could get in the way of his future plans for this city. But the moment that lowlife touched her hair...the aura of death Leonis kept concealed began slipping out, ever so slightly.

Not that I regret it.

Leonis was the most tolerant and lenient among the Dark Lords, but even that had its limits.

After all, *Riselia Crystalia was already his minion.*

"Miss Finé!"

"It looks like Muselle Rhodes has his eye on you. My condolences."

The girl approached the two of them. She was a beautiful young woman with sleek, black hair that could've been spun from the darkness of night itself. She was a bit taller than Riselia, and there was a mature air about her.

With a wave of the girl's arm, the orb of light that floated at her side disappeared into thin air. Was that orb a Holy Sword, too...?

"Thank you for your help, ma'am." Riselia bowed her head in gratitude.

The black-haired young woman shook her head and then squatted down to look at Leonis.

"So you're the boy she found in the ruin."

"Yes." Leonis nodded, feeling his pulse quicken.

...Did every girl Riselia knew have a big chest?

"I'm Elfiné Phillet. I serve as a platoon operator."

"Miss...Elfiné?"

Leonis remembered the name. She was the one Riselia had been communicating with earlier. Her voice was soothing, as if it was somehow enveloping him like a blanket.

"I'm Leonis Magnus. Miss Riselia rescued me in the ruin."

"Heh-heh. I suppose that makes you little Leo," she said, gently patting his head.

...Between her and Riselia, why did everyone seem so keen on shortening the Undead King's name?

"Welcome to Excalibur Academy. We greet you with open arms. I actually just received your uniform from the bureau. The size should be right, I think..."

She took a folded uniform set from her bag and handed it to Riselia.

"Thank you, ma'am."

"Are you going to have his Holy Sword registered next?"

"I thought I'd bring him to the dorm first. Have him take a bath and change."

"Oh, I see. You should probably take a bath, too, Selia."

"...Huh?! Do I smell...?" Shocked, Riselia sniffed at her sleeve. "Do I smell, Leo?!"

"Well, I didn't mind..."

"..." Riselia's shoulders dropped.

"Don't worry, you don't smell," Elfiné reassured her with a wry smile. "You're just dirty with sand."

"By the way, will you be going back to the dorm, too, ma'am?" Riselia asked.

"I have some Void investigation data I need to submit to the knights. There's definitely something below the sea in this sector."

"Something? Like ruins?"

"It's hard to tell. The knights have sent elite investigation teams to check it out, but..."

...*Under the sea, hmm?* The conversation caught Leonis's interest. The site of the Dark Lords' Armies' final battle sat here, below the ocean. Right beneath their feet...

CHAPTER 4

THE UNDEAD KING'S MINION

"This is the girls' dorm for our team."

Riselia's unit lived in the Hræsvelgr dorm. It was fairly removed from the center of Excalibur Academy, where most of the facilities were concentrated. Its appearance seemed to stand in contrast to the rectilinear designs of the city's buildings, being closer to the familiar sight of a noble's estate.

...Retro-culture, I believe it was called?

It likely used the architecture of the old kingdom of Londirk as its motif. Londirk was a great kingdom that once commanded corps of magical knights, but the nation eventually submitted to Leonis's army of the dead and swore fealty to him.

"Dorms are assigned according to a platoon's achievements," Riselia explained, pushing the door open.

"Platoon..."

...That guy, Muselle, had told Riselia to join his platoon.

"It's a tactical unit Holy Swordsmen deploy in. They're usually made up of five to six people," the girl continued.

She explained that Excalibur Academy organized platoons to fight Voids. Holy Swords had a wide variety of abilities, and so it was recommended that members with abilities that complemented and augmented each other team up and work together. There was no limitation on the members' gender or age, and it wasn't unusual for upperclassmen to partner up with younger students.

"The academy works on a complete merit system. Besides the missions platoons are sent on, there are training matches between Holy Swordsmen and all sorts of other tests. Platoons with high rankings get to stay in newer dorms. The Fafnir dorm has air conditioning, the newest workout equipment, a Jacuzzi, and even a sauna!"

"...I—I see."

Riselia was obviously quite passionate about the issue, but Leonis could muster little more than a vague response. He didn't have the faintest idea what a Jacuzzi was. Probably some sort of weapons system.

Riselia's room was up the stairs, on the second floor.

"Come in, make yourself at home..." Riselia stepped in first and motioned for him to follow.

"It might be a bit late to be asking this, but is it all right for me to be in a girls' dorm?"

"It's fine, Leo. You're still a kid."

Leonis wasn't sure what was so "fine" about it but entered all the same. The room was neatly furnished. There was a sofa arranged with cushions, a bed with neat sheets spread over it, and a wooden dining table sporting a porcelain teapot. Sitting on the windowsill was a pot with a decorative cactus.

It was quite different from the oppressive atmosphere of the Undead King's Death Hold.

"Being in your own room sure is relaxing..." The silver-haired girl sat on the edge of her bed and started taking off her knee socks.

I-I'm standing right here, you know...! Leonis thought, his heart skipping a beat despite himself. The glimpse of her healthy, shapely thighs peeking out from under the hem of her skirt was dazzling. *Maybe I should clear my throat to remind her I'm in the room...*

...But pointing that out would make it clear he was looking at her that way.

Wh-why am I getting so flustered?! I'm a Dark Lord; I need only confidently state my business!

And having convinced himself, Leonis averted his gaze slightly.

"Oh, Leo, you head into the bath first, okay?" Riselia pointed to a door as she started undoing the buttons on her blouse.

◆

Warm water poured over Leonis's skin, and white steam rose and clouded his vision. The bathroom attached to Riselia's room was surprisingly large. The boy knew of private baths like these, but they were reserved for nobles and royalty. Common people used public bathhouses or hot springs.

She does seem to be of noble birth...

Riselia had a personal maid and conducted herself with a refined gentility.

The shower's warm water rained down, drenching the Undead King's black hair.

This must be some magic apparatus employing water and fire sorcery...

Curious, he looked at the shower's stopper. It was engraved in the shape of a lion. It had been designed to work with even the tiniest mana reaction.

It was hard to believe something as advanced as this could exist while sorcery had been entirely forgotten.

In Leonis's day, sorcery was a unique power reserved for those with the talent to use it. But in this age, mankind had developed technologies that allowed almost anyone to make use of them.

...And thus sorcery, which requires natural ability, became unnecessary...

Sorcery was cast aside, but with the appearance of a new enemy—Voids—mankind developed a new weapon to oppose them: Holy Swords. An unusual power that differed from sorcery on a fundamental level.

...It likely wasn't a power that originated in this world.

He had nothing to confirm that, but the Dark Lord felt as much. Riselia had called it a gift the planet bestowed upon humanity.

But does the planet really have that kind of power...?

Voids, Holy Swords...everything was too different from the time with which Leonis was familiar. Even if he was to try rebuilding the Dark Lords' Armies, he lacked information about this world. A mistake now would do nothing but cause him more trouble.

More importantly, had *she* really been reincarnated into this world?

For the time being, I should wait for Shary and Blackas to return with their reports.

Leonis covered his hands in foamy soap and started rinsing his hair.

...Incidentally, I did hear something interesting back there.

He recalled the conversation he'd overheard a short while earlier. Large ruins were detected on the seabed below. Leonis happened to know exactly what those ruins were. This area was where Death Hold, Necrozoa's fortress, once stood. It was also the site of the final battle between the Six Heroes and the Dark Lords' Armies.

Which meant that below these waves slumbered the remains of countless undead and monsters, as well as the Archsage Arakael Degradios, the one who'd merged with the Holy Tree.

...The Archsage had a kind of immortality, too, but even he shouldn't have been able to survive on the ocean floor.

But the fact that Voids had spawned there was of interest.

Just a coincidence, perhaps? Or maybe...?

But just as the thought crossed his now foamy head...

"Leo, are you all right in there?"

"Yes, the water's just the right... Aaaah?!" Leonis reflexively turned toward the voice and let out a yelp.

Silvery hair fluttered from across the steamy room... Skin as white as virgin snow... A pair of breasts appeared before his eyes.

"...Aaah, erm...!"

Leonis almost knocked over a bucket.

"What's wrong, Leo?!" Riselia asked in surprise.

"Wh-why?!"

The Undead King fell, his bottom colliding with the tiled floor.

In his panic, he forgot to even cover his face with his hands, giving him a perfect view of her gorgeous nude form. Wet silvery locks clung to her bare skin. It was as if the goddess of the moon had descended to the earth.

"What, are you embarrassed at me seeing you naked? Boys shouldn't get embarrassed over that."

No, no, I'm not the one who should be embarrassed here...! The thought all but screamed in Leonis's mind.

...Maybe this was considered the norm in this weird post-one-thousand-year world?

...Perhaps this era's sense of decency differs from my time's as well!

Putting aside how odd it was for an Undead King to be hung up over decorum, Leonis was quite taken aback. His confusion caught Riselia's attention. She peered down at the boy.

"Aah!" she suddenly exclaimed.

"Wh-what is it...?" Leonis asked, a hint of fear in his voice.

"You're supposed to use shampoo for your hair, not soap!"

"...Huh?"

She frowned and sat Leonis down on a chair.

"You've got such pretty hair; you shouldn't damage it like that."

She poured hot water over his hair and began rinsing it.

"I can wash myself..."

"Noooope! Let your big sister handle it."

"...?!"

Leonis shut his eyes tight as he felt a bit of shampoo get into them.

"What lovely skin. It's hard to believe you didn't live in the city."

Riselia started rubbing his back with a sponge. This girl had the greatest of the Dark Lords completely at her mercy. Every now and then, Leonis felt a soft, squishy sensation against his back. As his pulse skyrocketed, he made conscious, pained efforts to not dwell on what the source of it might be. Riselia, on the other hand, didn't seem to mind pressing her skin against his at all.

Is this because of this child body, or...?

Whatever it was, the feeling of her slender fingers rinsing his hair was a pleasant one... Until her hands suddenly stopped.

"...Could I tell you a bit about myself?" she asked.

"Sure." Leonis nodded.

She turned off the shower water.

"...My parents were killed by Voids," she confided in a whisper. "They called it a Stampede—an unpredictable, large-scale disaster instigated by a Void that commanded others. It happened six years ago. My old home, the Third Assault Garden, was destroyed in a single night."

She went on to detail that her parents were Holy Swordsmen and commanders of the assault corps, and that they had died in the line of duty, defending the civilians. The only members of Crystalia house to survive were her and her maid, Regina.

"The search and rescue forces found us ten days later. It was expected that the daughter of two Holy Swordsmen would exhibit the same power, so I was admitted into Excalibur Academy. But..." Riselia trailed off into bitter silence.

"You can't produce a Holy Sword...?"

"...That's right." Riselia nodded. "What Muselle said is true. I haven't awakened the power of a Holy Sword."

According to Riselia, children with the factor that allowed one to produce a Holy Sword manifested at least part of the power at the age of ten at the earliest and fourteen at the latest. And in cases like Riselia's, where both parents were Holy Swordsmen, the chance of the child manifesting the power was nearly 90 percent.

But despite all her efforts, she couldn't summon a Holy Sword. She proactively went on ruin explorations, thinking that a weapon given to mankind to combat Voids might materialize more easily when fighting them.

"That's reckless..."

"...Y-yes... I know that." Riselia hung her head at Leonis's remark. "But if I don't awaken a Holy Sword soon, I'll lose my right to be here."

Her voice was tinged with anxiety and bitterness... Leonis understood how she felt perfectly. That feeling of wanting power more than anyone else but being unable to attain it. Just as he had once wished for the power to protect those dear to him.

"But I believe I'll eventually awaken a Holy Sword." Riselia clenched her fists to her chest.

"Erm, Leo..." Riselia's voice was now a whisper.

"What would you think of joining my platoon?"

"...Me, join your platoon?"

He felt her nod gently.

"Of course, you don't have to if you don't want to..." The young woman lowered her head. "You're free to join whichever platoon you like. Your Holy Sword can heal injuries, so I'm sure a lot of other units would want you..." Riselia sped through the words under her breath.

...Is this an attempt to recruit me?

"So that's why you've been employing your feminine wiles. Maybe I've misjudged you."

"F-feminine wi... N-n-no, that's not it at all!" Flustered, Riselia hurriedly pulled her body away from Leonis.

"I'm only joking," Leonis said. "But you couldn't fault me if I were to misunderstand, could you?"

"...You might have a cute face, but you're a bully on the inside." Riselia pouted.

...But Leonis knew she was a fair and honest person. It was why she had told him she couldn't use a Holy Sword before asking him.

A girl who couldn't manifest a Holy Sword... A girl on the verge of being cast out of the academy. Excepting people with ulterior motives like that scum, Muselle, there weren't many who'd see any benefit to teaming up with a girl like Riselia.

...Whatever happens, it was my intent to stick with her anyway.

After all, he would be better off having his minion at his side.

"...If you join our platoon, you'll always have tasty sweets whenever you want them."

"Trying to reel me in with food this time?"

"Th-that's not...!"

That's when it happened.

"H-huh...?"

Riselia staggered, as if hit by a sudden dizziness.

"Ah... Are you all right?" Leonis caught her by the shoulders.

She probably didn't realize this herself, but...her body was deathly cold, like a corpse.

"Ah, sorry, I...I'm suddenly feeling very weak..."

...Looks like she's about to reach her limit.

The girl's breathing rapidly became labored, and the light began fading from her ice-blue eyes. Leonis leaned her against the wall, so as to place her in a more comfortable position.

"I'm sorry. I lied to you."

"...Huh?" Riselia looked up at Leonis with a dazed expression.

"—What I used to heal you...wasn't the power of a Holy Sword, Selia."

What he'd done couldn't even rightly be considered healing. Because despite everything, she was already...

"Le...o...?"

"Riselia Crystalia is already dead."

♦

"L-Leo... What are you...saying...?" Riselia asked through labored breaths.

Her expression made it plain that the young woman hadn't grasped what the boy had said.

Well, I suppose it's only natural...

It pained Leonis to see Riselia in such a state. He averted his gaze as he continued to explain.

"There's no mistaking that a monster in the ruins killed you, Selia. And my power only governs over death, so I can't resurrect a life that's been lost."

It was true; the Undead King Leonis couldn't use holy magic. Therefore, he'd had to use magic from the Realm of Death to resurrect her as an undead.

"B-but I..."

"Unfortunately, you only seem to be alive." Leonis shook his head. "This seal is the proof."

"...?!"

A crimson seal surfaced on her thigh.

"What...is this...?"

"A tenth-order spell called Create Elder Undead. Honestly, it was a gamble whether it would succeed or not. It could have just as easily reduced you to ash or made you into a mindless ghoul..."

However, the actual result far exceeded the Undead King's expectations. A seal that shone bloodred only surfaced on those undead minions of the highest level and power...

"—You're a Vampire Queen. The highest rank possible for an undead being."

In order to become a Vampire Queen, one needed the kind of noble soul that was worthy of being a ruler of the night. It also required that the subject be a pure, unsullied maiden...

"A...ngh... Vampire... Khh, gaah...," Riselia moaned.

"Don't worry, it's just your mana reserves running low. Bear with it just a bit longer." Leonis knelt next to her.

Tracing the seal on her thigh with the tip of his finger, the boy let some of his massive mana reserves flow into it.

"...Aaah, mmm..." Riselia bit her lip, as if to suppress an indecent moan.

"Ah... Haaah... Nnn..."

The pale blue of Riselia's cloudy eyes turned a burning crimson. She gave an audible swallow.

"Aaah, nnn..."

Her first mana-shortage-induced vampiric impulse was an intense one. It wasn't a condition that could be controlled with any

kind of mental fortitude. Leonis stuck out his thumb at the girl. Riselia ran her tongue over it in a daze before sinking sharp teeth into the flesh.

"...Ugh..."

There was no pain, but Leonis contorted his face at the itchy sensation. Mana began coursing through the vampiress's body, transmitted via the Undead King's blood. Her silvery hair began to glow.

◆

After an hour or so, Riselia had finally calmed down. The newly supplied mana spurred her heart to beat again, and her temperature was gradually returning to normal.

"...Just who are you?" she asked, lying beneath her bedsheets.

Having calmed down, the reality of her undead existence was starting to sink in.

"I'm an ancient mage who was resurrected." Leonis gave a nod as he put on his uniform top.

He kept his status as the Undead King secret, instead explaining he was an ancient mage slumbering in the crystal Riselia had found, and he was capable of using the lost art of sorcery. He clarified that it was his magic that had turned her into his minion.

Riselia silently listened to the explanation before offering a question:

"Sorcery? Not a Holy Sword?"

"In the age I lived in, we used spells and sorcery."

"I see..."

It didn't seem she was wholly convinced yet, but...

Riselia took another look at her body.

"...All right. I'll believe you," the girl said with a small sigh. "It really does seem like I died..."

"I'm sorry. This was the only way I could save you with my magic."

"...I understand."

The young woman's shock was unmistakable, but the facts were plain as day. There was little to do but accept them. She came to terms with the situation quicker than Leonis had expected.

It's clear she still feels conflicted about it all, though...

That much was easy to understand.

Riselia huddled deeper beneath the covers.

"So I'm not human anymore, am I...?"

"That...would be the case, yes." It was unpleasant news for Leonis to have to relate.

"Do you think I'm still able to gain the power of a Holy Sword?"

"I don't know."

Leonis had no way of knowing about that unfamiliar power. However, he couldn't say for certain there was no chance, either.

"I see..." Riselia fell silent for a moment. "But you did save my life, right?"

".........."

Such a fair girl. She'd died to save Leonis, so it only made sense for him to return that kindness in some way. But even if he were to point that out, Riselia wouldn't hold it against him.

"...Then, yeah. I'm grateful," she said, hugging a pillow.

"Huh?"

"I'm better off this way than dying down in the ruins, right?"

"Well, I suppose so, but..." The greatest Dark Lord found himself a bit taken aback.

"...All right. Then it's settled."

Riselia rose to her feet, resigned to her new circumstances, sheets still clenched in her fingers.

"By the way, are you after something? Why were you asleep all those years?"

"Well..." Leonis fell silent for a few moments, carefully picking his words. "There's someone I'm looking for."

"Someone?" Riselia seemed to sense something in the boy's earnest tone. "Is this person...important to you?"

"Yes." Leonis nodded.

"I see. All right, then." Riselia beamed at him. "Then I'll help you find that someone."

"I appreciate it, but..."

"But in exchange..." Riselia stuck out her index finger. "I want you to make me stronger. Strong enough to fight the Voids."

"That shouldn't be too difficult." Leonis was by no means opposed to strengthening his minions.

"In that case, I look forward to working with you, Leo."

And so the Undead King and his vampire minion sealed the agreement with a handshake.

CHAPTER 5

THE HOLY SWORD TRIAL

It was thus that Leonis made Riselia his minion...

Before going to the administration bureau for what was called a Holy Sword Trial, the two of them stopped for a light meal. At any rate, Leonis wasn't undead anymore. He'd need sustenance, or he wouldn't be able to use his sorcery properly.

"What would you do if I exposed your identity to the bureau?"

"...I'm not worried about that."

If Riselia were to expose him, it would also come out that she was a vampire. That wasn't an option for someone who aspired to be a Holy Swordswoman.

"...I—I know," Riselia murmured grumpily.

"Regardless, a minion can't betray its master." A seal surfaced on Leonis's hand, and he presented it to the young woman.

"What's that?"

"A seal of dominion and subordination. It can be used to force a minion to obey—"

"N-no...! You mean, like, pervy things, too?!" Tears welled up in Riselia's eyes.

"...Well, it's possible. I won't do anything like that, though."

"...R-really?"

"Really," answered Leonis, a bit exasperated.

...Some Dark Lords were known to use minions for such purposes. As the Undead King, Leonis had never subjected his minions to such treatment.

"...All right. I believe you, Leo." Riselia nodded. "You were a gentleman when we were in the bath together. But what is a minion supposed to do?"

"A minion's purpose in being is to defend their master, since this body has grown weak..."

Riselia giggled at his words.

"Don't worry, your big sister will keep you safe." The girl patted his head somewhat happily.

The two then entered one of the school's restaurants and claimed a table.

...*A human body really is troublesome.*

Leonis's feelings had entirely flipped since his time in the bath. The newly undead Riselia, on the other hand, looked a bit anxious.

"Hey, I'm not really that hungry, but I can still eat normally, right?"

"Higher-ranking vampires can eat regular food, yes. It takes time to convert the nutrients into mana, though, so it's a bit inefficient." Leonis spoke in a whisper. "Also, unlike most vampires, you can walk around in daytime."

A Vampire Queen was among the highest grade of undead creatures, rivaling even Elder Liches and Black Knights. It was a High Daywalker, dissimilar from the Nightwalker species of undead.

"...Oh, thank goodness." Riselia sighed in relief.

A vampire who ate food was also useful in terms of camouflage.

"Erm, if you ever really feel to urge to drink blood, feel free to take it from me."

He may have done it to save her life, but he'd still turned this girl who aspired to be a Holy Swordswoman into a vampire. The least he could do was share his blood whenever she needed it.

But when he said it, Riselia made a small, barely audible gulping sound.

"........."

Her ice-blue eyes were fixed intently on the nape of Leonis's neck.

"...Um. Just a bit, though, all right?"

"N-no, that's not what I...!" The girl turned away, her face flushing as red as a tomato. "I won't drink blood, and I don't want to forget my humanity."

"...Ah, keep your voice down...!" Leonis looked around the nearby tables, flustered.

Thankfully, they'd come in at around three in the afternoon, so there weren't too many students about. What few there were eyed their table and seemed to be whispering to one another.

...Did they hear what we just said?

He used a Sensory Expansion spell to listen in on their conversation.

"Check him out! Isn't that kid, like, super cute?"

"Uhhh. He's still small. Are you into that or something?"

"Yeah! Gotta pick 'em when they're young and fresh."

"Whoa, you've got a serious criminal vibe. When kids that cute grow up, they become Dark Lords in the bedroom, know what I mean?"

"Stop it, that sounds bad... Ah, he looked over here. ♪"

One of the girls gave a mischievous smile and waved at him... which Leonis promptly ignored. Hearing the words *Dark Lord* did make his heart skip a beat, though.

"Watch what you're saying...," he warned Riselia.

The silver-haired girl hid her face awkwardly behind the menu.

"So did you decide what you'll order?" she asked.

"...Bread will do."

"Bread...? You mean this freshly baked bread?"

"Yes, that."

"There's lots of other stuff you could try. The food in this cafeteria is pretty good," she said, pointing at a few menu items.

"Bread will do just fine. I don't really know what all these other things are...," Leonis said, cocking his head dubiously.

What is all this? Gratin...lasagna, pasta...?

These were all dishes Leonis had never heard of before. They likely didn't exist a thousand years ago. Or maybe they did but only adorning the tables of royalty and nobility. Whichever it was, they certainly hadn't been part of Leonis's world.

Riselia suddenly poked Leonis's forehead with her index finger.

"Just bread simply isn't enough. You need balanced nutrition."

"I'd rather not have an undead preach to me about nutr— Ah."

By the time he stopped himself, it was already too late.

"...Nnnnn...!"

Tears began forming in Riselia's eyes.

"I—I get it, okay? I'm sorry!"

Leonis offered a hurried apology. A Dark Lord begging his minion for forgiveness was an odd sight to be sure, but it wasn't like she'd willingly become undead.

"...Meanie," Riselia whispered sullenly.

"...I'm sorry," Leonis apologized again, which she regarded with a little sniff.

"In that case, try this season's vegetable-garnished pasta. Okay?"

"Fine, I'll have that." Leonis nodded.

Riselia ordered them the pasta and a salad.

"Your big sister will cover for you today. Once they issue your permanent ID card, use your own credits, okay?"

"Credits?"

"That's the currency we use in the Assault Gardens. Completing tasks for the academy earns you rewards."

"Oh, money. I see..."

Leonis smiled boastfully and pulled a gold coin from his shadow. It was a large Reidoa gold coin, issued by the Schkarest Empire. A commoner could live for the rest of his or her life off one of these coins, and Leonis had over twenty thousand of them hidden away in the Realm of Shadows. He'd taken them as military funds from Necrozoa's vaults, planning to use them for the upcoming revival of the Dark Lords' Armies.

However...

"...What? What is this...?"

Riselia's reaction to seeing the coin was lacking, to say the least.

"Huh...? It's a Reidoa coin. One of these is worth enough to buy this entire restaurant."

"Well, erm... I don't think they take that kind of money here...," Riselia said with a mixed expression. "The Seventh Assault Garden only accepts credits."

"Wh-what...?" Leonis was dumbstruck. "B-but even if I can't use it as currency, isn't pure gold rare and valuable...?"

"Oh, it's pure gold. But gold isn't that rare of a metal." Riselia smiled at him cheerily.

"Huh...?"

"It's used in decoration, but... Actually, the gold we refine is probably even purer than this."

"..."

In an instant, the vast troves of wealth amassed in the Treasury of Shadows became worthless.

Leonis could only moan in despair.

But as he did...

"Oh, is that an old coin? Classy thing you've got there."

A voice, cool like the wind, reached Leonis's ears. Turning around, he was faced with a girl curiously eyeing the coin in his hand. Her hair was a shade of azure reminiscent of the sky.

She wore her hair short. At first glance, one might mistake her for a beautiful young man. However, her plump chest made a clear outline below her white outfit. She was short, just a bit taller than Leonis's ten-year-old body. Her outfit was different from Riselia's. The top of her uniform was casually draped over some sort of eccentric getup. Her eyes held the calm composure of a gorgeous young woman.

"Ah, Sakuya..." Riselia raised her eyes to meet Sakuya's and waved.

...They're acquainted, from the looks of things.

"Isn't there a tactical drill today?"

"Yeah, but it was painfully boring. I snuck out," the short-haired beauty said and then turned her gaze to Leonis. "Are you the boy capable of using a Holy Sword...?"

"You've heard about Leo?"

"Yes, Miss Elfiné told me about him. You were found in a ruin, right?"

"Yes, I was abducted by the Voids until Selia saved me..."

"Hmm. Well, whatever happened, it's a good thing you're safe." The short-haired girl silently extended her right hand. "I'm Sakuya Sieglinde. Nice to meet you."

"Leonis Magnus." Leonis returned the handshake.

Her hand was small and slightly cold. Unmistakably a girl's hand. But the moment he grasped it, Leonis realized something.

...This is the hand of one who lives by the sword.

She looked to be about fourteen or fifteen years old. Just how much training had she endured to reach such a level at this age...?

"Hmm, Leo, is it? A good name. Invokes the image of a lion." The girl smiled, letting go of his hand.

"Sakuya is our platoon's vanguard attacker," Riselia explained.

...I see, they're in the same platoon.

Leonis was genuinely curious as to how Riselia had managed to tempt a swordswoman like Sakuya to her side.

"By the way, are you two here for lunch?"

"Yes. We're going to eat and then go register Leo's Holy Sword."

"Hmm. Sorry if I'm interrupting, then."

"You're not interrupting anything, Sakuya. Have you had lunch yet?"

"Mmm, well..." Sakuya averted her gaze and fell silent for a moment. "I actually don't have any credits on me today."

"What? What did you waste all your credits on?!" Riselia raised her voice in surprise.

"Gambling."

"...So it's your own fault."

"It is."

Riselia reached a cold conclusion, to which Leonis nodded and agreed.

"...Th-that's wrong!" Sakuya shook her head defensively. "I just, well, I got a little fired up, and..."

"........." Riselia's scrutiny grew sharper.

...Contrary to how cool and collected this Sakuya person looked, she was pretty hopeless.

"I ran out of credits, so the other party agreed they'd let me off the hook if I showed them my breasts. I was about to take off my shirt when a professor on patrol walked in..."

"S-Sakuya! Y-you can't do that—you're a girl!" Riselia grabbed Sakuya by the shoulders and started shaking her.

"No sweat. The other person was a girl, too."

"...I, uh, does that make it any better?" Riselia wondered with a perplexed expression.

Sakuya did have an appearance that looked like it might be popular among girls, too, but...

"Anyway, one thing led to another, and I'm broke." The words almost sounded boastful coming from Sakuya.

Riselia give a small sigh.

"What am I going to do with you? Fine, I'll treat you to lunch."

"No, Miss Riselia, I couldn't..."

"It's fine. I got some credits from the ruin investigation." The silver-haired girl presented her card.

"Then I owe you one. Truthfully, my stomach's been growling quite a bit for a while now." Sakuya bowed her head deeply and politely took a seat at their table.

"What did you order, kid?"

"Some food I've never heard of before."

"A daredevil, are you? I think I'll go for some pancakes."

"Sakuya, you can't live on just sweets," Riselia chimed in.

"You've absolutely nothing to worry about. I won't gain any weight."

"That's not what I...," Riselia said, holding her temples in a gesture of exhaustion.

As they waited for their dishes to arrive, Leonis brought up a question that bothered him.

"Erm... Miss Sakuya, what's that outfit you're wearing?"

"Oh, this? It's my homeland's...the traditional garb of the Sakura Orchid." Sakuya nodded. "...It's a memento of my elder sister."

Sakuya's expression instantly turned serious. Leonis swore he could see a black flame burning in her eyes.

"My village's clan was killed by the Voids," she said in a chillingly cold voice. "Slaying those things is my calling."

Her tone was filled with such cold determination that it made students from the nearby tables turn and look. Leonis had seen a few people with that same fire burning in their eyes before.

...*She's one who seeks vengeance.*

"Sakuya...," Riselia said with a solemn voice.

And...

"Sorry, this isn't a story I should be telling someone I just met." Sakuya shrugged, as if to relax herself.

"No, I shouldn't have pried."

"My appearance violates school regulation, but there's no way I wouldn't wear this tribute to my sister. I got special permission."

"Sakuya has very high records for slaying Voids on solo missions. She's one of the few students to achieve that during their earlier years at the academy."

"It's not all that great... Oh, here they come."

A waiter walked up to take their orders, and Leonis ordered the season's vegetable-garnished pasta.

◆

The pasta ended up being very much to Leonis's taste. Mankind's cuisine seemed to have greatly evolved in the last thousand years. They now boasted a much larger variety of seasonings. Sakuya Sieglinde returned to her dorm, saying she needed to pawn some of her things.

...Leonis couldn't help but wonder if a gambler at her age would really be all right.

Leaving the restaurant, Leonis was led to the academy's training grounds. The place was a maze of training facilities used for a variety of different purposes. The complex was large enough to fit two or maybe three castles from Leonis's era.

These grounds alone are vast enough to raise an army of ten thousand skeleton warriors...

Waiting for them there was a woman in a military uniform, standing with her hands on her hips.

"Right on time. Good. I'm Diglassê Alto, the instructor in charge of your trial."

"I'm Leonis Magnus."

"...The boy rescued from the ruins, yes?" The woman looked him over, seemingly appraising him. "You don't have to be so tense. The trial is only meant to confirm what type of Holy Sword you have."

"Type?"

"They register your Holy Sword's ability so they can adjust your training curriculum to suit it," Riselia explained.

Since Holy Swords had varied abilities, a uniform curriculum would be ineffective in developing them. Therefore, Holy Swordsmen officers had to examine each sword with their own eyes and make decisions as to what kind of training would be best.

"Yes, that's how it works. Now, could you show me your Holy Sword?"

"Understood. Come forth, Staff of Sealed Sins!" called Leonis.

His staff appeared from his shadow and settled in his hand.

"So your Holy Sword takes the shape of a staff. What type of abilities does it have?"

"Hmm... It's a support type, I suppose. It exhibits different powers depending on the situation." Leonis gave a vague sort of answer to describe everything his magic could do.

"I see. An all-purpose support type...," Diglassê said, inputting something into the tablet device in her hands. "All right. Could you show me your power?"

She fiddled with the pad, and a lump of metal sitting at the edge of the training grounds sprang to life. It was eight-legged and had a spiderlike form. Shining red mana crystals, each the size of a fist, were fixed at the joints where the legs met the body of the automaton.

"What's that?"

"A Void Simulator developed for training purposes by the magitech department," Riselia said. "It's programmed to fight like a Void would."

"We've set its performance to a low setting for the trial. Try fighting it."

"...Understood."

...What is this toy?

Leonis lifted his staff with a hint of displeasure.

I'll just fire a second-order Destructive Gravity Shot and be done with it...

He wanted to put this pointless formality behind him as soon as possible. With a grand flourish of his staff, the Undead King unleashed the gravity-type spell.

Voooooooooom!

The Void Simulator was crushed to bits with a deafening sound.

"...?!"

Diglassê and Riselia looked on in shock.

...Damn, did I overdo it?

"Y-you crushed a Void Simulator made of Metahalcum to bits...?"

"D-didn't you say your Holy Sword was a multipurpose support type? What was that just now...?!"

"I, erm, guess I hit it in a weak spot?"

"It seems like a lot more than just that! I'll need to check your Holy Sword more thoroughly!" Diglassê glared at Leonis.

...Not good. All I did was make her suspicious.

"Now, what should I use for the next trial...?"

No sooner had the words left the woman's lips, than...

"Wait just a moment," a familiar voice cut in.

A thin blond man surrounded by a group of girls approached them. Muselle Rhodes.

"What is it, Viscount Muselle? We're in the middle of a trial here." Instructor Diglassê narrowed her eyes at him, clearly displeased at his interruption.

Muselle merely smirked in response, approaching Leonis.

"Instructor, would you mind if I handled his trial?"

"What?" Diglassê furrowed her brow. "Viscount, need I remind you that unofficial duels are forbidden at the academy?"

"I'm not proposing a duel here, but a trial. With your approval, there should be no problems. Being a top-rank Holy Swordsman, I'm more than qualified."

There was a sadistic smile on Muselle's lips. It was clear he was looking for payback.

"...Boy, did you do anything to him?" Diglassê asked in a whisper, looking down at Leonis.

"...No," the boy answered.

Diglassê shrugged at his feigned ignorance.

"Hmm."

The woman glanced at the ruined Void Simulator. Clearly realizing something, her lips curved into a knowing smirk.

"Well, I suppose there's no harm, given how the simulator is broken and all."

...This woman's using this to gauge my power.

He'd unintentionally caught her interest with what he'd done earlier.

Fine, so be it..., Leonis thought with a sort of tired resignation.

"I don't mind. Assuming Mr. Muselle here can fill in for that ruined scrap heap."

"...What did you just say, brat?!" The blond young man's complacent expression easily gave way to anger.

He had to be a truly weak man to fall for such an obvious taunt.

Having this guy pick fights over and over could get tiresome...

Leonis thought this could be a chance to thoroughly crush him publicly.

"Leo, what are you doing?!" Riselia raised her voice in shock, but...

"I'll have you eat those words...! Hey!" At Muselle's signal, the four girls with whom he'd arrived drew their weapons.

Two of them held swords, another a mace, and the last carried a lance. Likely all Holy Swords. They moved in a manner devoid of will, like marionettes on strings.

"That's four on one! It's not fair!" Riselia protested.

"That's the power of my Holy Sword—Dominion, the Staff of Absolute Obedience. These four are an extension of my weapon."

Muselle produced a short staff in the shape of a conductor's baton.

So that's his Holy Sword...

"That's still not...!" Riselia looked to Diglassê.

The instructor simply shrugged again and shook her head.

...It was obvious she found this interesting on some level.

"I suppose I can understand that...," Leonis said in response to his opponent.

His army of undead was an extension of his own power. It stood to reason that anyone under the sway of this young man's

Holy Sword would be considered part of his power in much the same fashion.

"Leo..."

"I just need to defeat him and those four girls, right?" asked the Undead King.

"That's right," answered Diglassê with a nod.

"Wait. If that's the case, I'm fighting alongside him," Riselia interjected. "I'm Leo's minion...his guardian."

"Selia—"

"Pfft... Ah-ha-ha-ha! Fine by me!" Muselle's face contorted in amusement.

Judging by his expression, it seemed he'd counted on Riselia interfering.

"But I have a condition," he added.

"What?"

"If you lose, you have to join my platoon."

"...What?!"

"I'm agreeing to take a handicap here, so I should be allowed to set that as my condition."

"...!" Riselia ground her teeth in frustration.

Joining his platoon meant becoming like the girls who followed him around, and Riselia was well aware of the twisted lust Muselle harbored for her... What would become of her was obvious. It would only be natural for her to hesitate here...

"Fine." Leonis was the one to answer.

"...Huh?"

"But if you lose, Mr. Muselle"—Leonis pointed a finger in Muselle's direction—"you have to stop picking fights with Selia."

He intentionally called her Selia and not Riselia to provoke his opponent.

"...Ugh. Fine. I swear to it on my Holy Sword."

"Leo...," Riselia whispered, a little nervous.

"I have no intention of letting him lay a hand on my minion," Leo whispered back.

The silver-haired young woman nodded, seemingly having made up her mind as well.

It'd come about as an unexpected interruption, but this would be a good chance for him to test Riselia's power as his new undead minion.

And meanwhile, I'll play the role of support to do away with the instructor's suspicions.

"Instructor, could you lend me a training sword?"

"Sure. Feel free to use it." Diglassê tossed a rodlike weapon in Riselia's direction.

When Riselia caught it, the blade lit up.

"What's that?"

"An Artificial Relic, a replica of a Holy Sword, made for training purposes. It's not effective against Voids, but..."

Leonis understood. It was a weapon that used mana.

"Do you have experience with swordsmanship?"

She'd used a ranged weapon in the ruins, so Leonis was a bit surprised by her choice here.

"...I've kept my skills sharp for when my Holy Sword finally manifests." She showed off a few practice swings.

Her form was indeed well honed.

"A Holy Sword takes the shape of your soul. I thought if mine were to manifest, it should be in the shape of a sword."

Riselia stepped forward, gripping the training weapon in both hands.

"I'll act as vanguard, and you'll be support. All right, Leo?"

The boy nodded in reply.

Looking around, he saw a small crowd of onlookers had

gathered at some point. Apparently, a duel between Holy Swords-men during a trial was quite the show.

"Regulations are the same as the usual training matches. If someone loses consciousness or they yield, they're declared the loser. If I feel there's any danger to anyone's life, I also have the authority to end the battle then and there."

"So they just have to say they yield, right?" A vicious smirk was plastered on Muselle's face.

"Now let this duel of Holy Swords begin!"

With Diglassê's words, the duel trial commenced.

♦

The instant the battle started...

"Haaaaaaaaaah!"

A battle cry rang out. Riselia kicked off against the ground and charged forward. She moved swiftly toward the girl closest to her and went on the offensive.

Oh?

Leonis raised an eyebrow in surprise. Becoming a vampire may have boosted the girl's physical abilities, but her skills with a sword were more than just practiced. Her movements had obviously been well rehearsed and were backed by rigorous training.

The lance-wielding girl staggered, taking a blow to her torso. Riselia took another step forward and thrust the tip of her training blade against the girl's chest. At that moment, Riselia's mana burst outward, sending the other girl flying.

"Ooooh!" came the cry of the spectators.

"...What?!" Muselle cursed in surprise.

It seemed the fact that Riselia couldn't use a Holy Sword had made him underestimate her actual skills.

"Got you!" She charged at Muselle.

His Holy Sword had the ability to control other people. It only made sense she'd try to take him down quickly.

"Kuh... Inferior fool!"

Muselle blocked the aerial slash crashing toward him with his short staff.

...I see. So he wasn't all talk. He's agile and skilled in his own right.

The attack may have had some mana to it, but it was still only a training sword. It wasn't a match for the strength of a weapon that was the manifestation of its wielder's soul. The blond boy easily deflected the blow.

"Your swordsmanship lacks elegance!" Riselia called.

"Shut up!"

Riselia brandished her training sword and prepared to press on him again, when...

"...What are you doing?! Protect me!"

Muselle's staff lit up, taking command of one of the girls.

The puppet wielding a broadsword shoved herself between Riselia and Muselle, her face expressionless and without a trace of a will of her own.

"...Don't listen to that idiot...!"

"You're wasting your breath," Muselle said with a sneer. "They all willingly made a pact with my Holy Sword."

...So he isn't completely forcing them to obey.

These girls chose to become his weapons; Excalibur Academy wouldn't have approved of it any other way. During battle, Muselle acted as conductor and unified their wills. That, too, was a viable strategy.

...It's a mutually beneficial relationship. Or maybe they all genuinely have affection for this guy...hard as that may be to believe.

As Leonis calmly analyzed the situation, he felt a sharp gaze at his back. It was Instructor Diglassê, studying him intently, her tablet tight in her grasp.

...Oh, I nearly forgot this was my Holy Sword Trial. I was too preoccupied assessing my minion's power. Now, what shall I do...?

Reducing that man to ashes would be easy, but it would expose the truth about Leonis... And killing Muselle could cause its own troubles.

...I guess I'll try to just make a moderate impression.

Leonis swung his staff and began chanting a spell. Taking notice, Muselle stepped away from Riselia and issued an order to his followers.

"Hey! Take out the kid!"

The lance-wielding girl Riselia had knocked back earlier jumped to her feet and charged the boy.

"...Leo!" Riselia broke her focus for a moment.

"I'm fine! Focus on him, Selia!" Leonis jumped back, still chanting his spell.

Right now, Leonis only had the athleticism of a ten-year-old. His body held a great deal of potential, as it belonged to a former hero. However, his soul was that of a Dark Lord, which seemed to generate some kind of interference. Leonis couldn't quite move as he intended.

Having judged her target's abilities as inferior, the lance-wielding girl was closing in fast.

"Come forth, the deceased of the Realm of Shadows—Shadow Hand, Mesta Mord!"

"Aaah!"

Shadow hands coiled around the charging girl's legs, making her trip and topple to the ground.

Diglassê's eyes widened in surprise.

At that same moment, he also conjured several strengthening

spells, chanted at the same time, to silently augment Riselia's ability. They were all first-order spells: Agility, Protection of the Spirits, and Sensory Expansion.

...I suppose this much assistance should do.

Leonis did his best to keep his mana to a minimum. He wondered if Blackas might mock him for being overprotective of his minions...

With Leonis's strengthening magic assisting her, Riselia's movements hastened. She easily defeated the mace-wielding girl who stood in her way. Her next slash brought down the girl with the broadsword. She sprinted between the Holy Swordswomen with superhuman speed.

She still seemed to be slightly overwhelmed by her own vampiric powers, but she bested her opponents all the same. Only a single girl wielding a shortsword remained to protect Muselle.

"Do you intend to just scurry around while using girls as your shield, Muselle Rhodes?!" Riselia taunted provocatively, eliciting enthusiastic cheers from the crowd.

It seemed the young man wasn't very popular among his peers.

"That's right!"

"Quit running, Muselle!"

"Take him out!"

"...Lady Selia?!"

Oh?

A familiar voice was mixed in with the cheers.

Leonis turned around, looking up at the second-floor balcony of the facility. There he saw Regina, her blond pigtails blowing in the wind. Riselia didn't seem to notice her, though.

"Tch!" Muselle clicked his tongue and held up his staff.

It seemed his intention had been to derive sadistic pleasure from tormenting Riselia in front of Leonis for not having a Holy

Sword of her own. Things had gone quite differently than the blond young man had expected, however.

...He would never imagine she's actually a Vampire Queen.

"Don't underestimate me! Or the power of my Dominance!" A light erupted from Muselle's staff.

...What?

Riselia suddenly froze, just a step away from Muselle.

"...!"

Muselle's staff lit up as if in a roar, and each of the girls' Holy Swords shone in response.

"Activate!" "Activate!" "Activate!" "Activate!"

"You forcibly drew the power out of their Holy Swords?!"

"Playtime's over!" cried Muselle, a cruel grin spreading across his face.

""""Hyaaaah!""""

The girls wielding the shortsword, mace, and broadsword charged at Riselia. But this time, they weren't expressionless. They were in a complete frenzy.

"—Rock Break!"

The girl right in front of Riselia swung down hard with her shining mace Holy Sword. The force of the attack exploded outward, shattering the stone floor of the training grounds.

...Not bad. That looked fairly powerful, Leonis thought, impressed.

It matched a second-order spell, the Rock Burst spell Blag, in firepower. In other words, it was powerful enough to kill a person if it landed a direct hit...

Leonis glanced in Diglassê's direction, but the woman showed no particular reaction to what had happened. This much was apparently an everyday occurrence at Excalibur Academy.

"Yaaah! Lightning Charge!"

The lance-wielding girl who'd been pinned by Leonis's Mesta

Mord spell loosed the power of her Holy Sword. Even so, the light-ning bolt she fired wasn't strong enough to break through Leonis's sorcerous defense. He snapped his fingers, and more shadows envel-oped the girl.

"...Whoa, what's that?!"

"That's pretty grim for a kid."

"I wonder what Holy Sword he has..."

Leonis realized he was drawing the crowd's attention, but hon-estly, he didn't care. He returned his attention to Riselia's fight. With the three girls having tapped the true power of their Holy Swords, she was visibly struggling.

"—Aerial Smash!"

The dagger-wielding student unleashed her attack, hitting Riselia right in the chest. Her petite body was blown back, rebound-ing several times against the ground before skidding to a halt.

"...Kuh... Ugh...!"

"Ah-ha-ha, yes, that's the expression I wanted to see you make."

Riselia made a pained sound as Muselle watched her, ecstatic. "Let's show that cheeky brat just how worthless you a— Ahhh!"

Muselle's body suddenly twitched in terror.

...Damn. I let my bloodlust show for a moment, and he took notice.

"...Aaah, Meiya, why are you having so much trouble with him?! He's just one kid! Crush him!" The young man aimed his Holy Sword staff in the direction of the girl bound by shadows.

"Don't bother," the Undead King said with a shrug.

The lance-wielding puppet could struggle as hard as she pleased but would never escape.

"...Ugh, does your Holy Sword control shadows?" Muselle asked, eyeing Leonis as if he were looking at something disgusting.

Then it happened.

"...n't...rt...!"

Riselia drove the training sword to the ground and staggered to her feet.

"What...?" Muselle's face twisted with displeased surprise.

He never expected her to get back up after taking a blow from a Holy Sword.

And yet...

"This...doesn't even hurt!"

Her silvery hair shone brilliantly with an intense surge of mana, and her ice-blue eyes had been drenched the color of blood. Riselia Crystalia was a Vampire Queen—the strongest of all undead. She may not have awakened yet, but the amount of mana in her body far surpassed that of a human.

"You dirty, cheating...!" Riselia practically flew across the field as she ran, her body enveloped with mana. The three girls wielding Holy Swords stood and rushed to protect Muselle. Riselia's sword flashed through the air, clashing against the mace wielded by one of Muselle's pawns.

"—Water Jail!"

Perhaps concluding they wouldn't match Riselia in brute strength, the girl with the broadsword released the power of her Holy Sword. A prison of water formed out of thin air, swallowing Riselia.

"...This is... Gah, pah...!"

"Ah-ha, ah-ha-ha-ha, how do you like the power of Millis's water-type Holy Sword?!" Muselle laughed loudly.

But his confident expression quickly crumbled.

"I told you...I won't lose!"

Mana surged from Riselia's body, forming winglike appendages as she broke through her watery cage.

"...This can't be...!"

Riselia swung her training sword with all her might, knocking the girl standing in her way out cold. She kept charging forward, flicking the shortsword-wielding girl off to the side as she went. There were no more marionettes left to protect Muselle. But as she closed in on him...

"...?!"

She froze just as she was about to bring down her training sword.

"...Wh-why...?!" she whispered with a wavering voice.

The training sword fell to the ground with a dry, clattering sound. The tip of Muselle's Holy Sword was thrust in front of her forehead.

"Heh, heh-heh... I don't know where you got that kind of power, but..." Muselle wore a confident grin. "In the end, it's no match for a true Holy Sword!"

"U... Ugh...!" Riselia stood stiff as a statue, incapable of moving.

What did he do?

Muselle laughed, as if to answer Leonis's question.

"This is the power of my Staff of Absolute Obedience—Forced Dominion!"

Muselle picked up the training sword Riselia had dropped and hit her over the head with it.

"Ugh, aaah...!" Riselia fell to the ground, incapable of resisting.

"This is all your fault, Riselia. You should have obeyed me!"

He beat her over and over as she lay there, unable to get up.

"What's wrong, brat?! You're just going to watch?!" Muselle taunted.

"Hey, cut it out!" "Is bullying a weak student that fun?" "She can't even move!"

Spectators raised their voices in complaint. However, Diglassê made no move to break up the fight.

This has gone on long enough, I suppose..., thought Leonis.

As Riselia's master, he could not allow this to continue.

I've seen enough. She may be inexperienced, but she shows promise nonetheless...

Holding up his staff, he began chanting his spell.

I suppose I should hold back, even against a bastard like him. At least so as to not completely wipe him out...

He was still willing to take an arm or two as payback for the way Muselle had toyed with his minion. But then...Leonis noticed. Riselia's eyes hadn't submitted yet.

"...ver, lose..."

"Huh?"

"Even without a Holy Sword, I'll never, ever lose to you!"

"What?!"

Riselia rose to her feet.

"It can't be... How did you break through my Forced Dominion?!" The blond boy staggered back a few steps, shock in his gaze. "Grr... Pointless resistance!"

He called upon the power of his Forced Dominion a second time...

But...

Every pair of eyes in the vicinity turned to Riselia as if time had stopped.

"...Huh?"

But no one was more surprised than Riselia herself. As she stood...a single sword appeared before her, shining with a solemn light. A shortsword so beautiful, one could only look upon it with silent respect. Its grip displayed beautiful craftsmanship.

"It can't...be... This is..." Riselia's eyes widened as she grabbed the hilt. The Holy Sword suited her perfectly, as if she'd wielded it all her life.

"...A Holy Sword?! That's impossible!" Muselle cried out in a panic.

There was no mistaking it. This was a Holy Sword born of Riselia's soul.

"Whoooooooooooooo!"

The surrounding students cheered.

"Ooh. Many awaken their Holy Swords in the heat of battle, but that daughter of the Crystalia family sure pulled off one dramatic summoning...," Leonis overheard Diglassê whispering to herself. "Wonder if it's got anything to do with meeting that boy?"

She cast a suspicious glance at Leonis. He simply looked away, turning his gaze back to his servant. Their eyes met, and she nodded before swinging her Holy Sword.

"—This is the power of my Holy Sword!"

"...So what?! Do you think you can beat me with a newly awakened Holy S—"

In a flash, the sound of torn air whistled. Riselia had disappeared from Muselle's sight.

"—Huh?"

The next moment, Riselia stood right behind him. Muselle's Holy Sword had broken in two and dissipated into particles of light.

"Ah... Aaah... M-my... My Holy Sword...!"

Leonis could hear the moment Muselle's heart broke.

"...What will you do?" Riselia asked, lowering the edge of her blade to his neck.

"S-submit! I submit!" Muselle exclaimed, raising both hands in the air.

Great cheers erupted from all directions around the victorious young woman.

"Lady Selia!" Regina ran down from the platform and embraced her friend.

"Congratulations, Riselia Crystalia," Diglassê said with a gentle smile. "Your efforts have at last been rewarded."

CHAPTER 6

A WELCOME PARTY

Pop, pop, pop pop pop!

The crisp sound of party poppers filled the common room of the girls' dorms.

"To Leo's admission to the eighteenth platoon, and to Lady Selia awakening her Holy Sword!" Regina made her toast dressed in a full maid's uniform, lifting a glass of nonalcoholic champagne.

True to her profession, she wore the outfit quite comfortably. She looked like a completely different person from the girl who blasted Voids with cannon fire.

"...Th-thank you," Leonis said, streamers from one of the party poppers tangled in his hair.

It was a surprise welcome party. The table in front of Leonis was full of tasty food and sweets.

"Regina prepared this as soon as she returned to the city," Riselia said, exposing the plan.

"On your instructions, Lady Selia. You said he'd definitely join our platoon."

...So that's why she went off on her own. Maybe Selia really did try to tempt me with candy.

"Plus, you were really something during your Holy Sword Trial. Promising, aren't you?" Sakuya smiled, sitting on the sofa opposite him.

"My Holy Sword is nothing all that special. It's just a support-type." Leonis shook his head. "Miss Selia's Holy Sword decided the match."

"Leo...," Riselia said bashfully, but there was a definite pride in her expression.

And who could fault her for it? She'd honed her skill with the sword, putting in every possible effort, all for the day when she would summon a Holy Sword. And today was that day.

"Yeah. The planet certainly rewarded you for your diligence today, Miss Selia. I'm happy for you," Sakuya said.

"Rumors about your Holy Sword are already roaring through the academy like wildfire."

"H-huh? Really?!"

"Of course. I asked the public relations department to spread the word, after all!"

"H-hey, you shouldn't have done that!"

Regina gave a teasing look and puffed up her chest boastfully. Riselia grabbed her sleeve.

Still, I don't think her awakening during the trial, of all times, was just coincidence..., Leonis thought as he watched the two girls sparring.

Riselia always had the talent to manifest a Holy Sword, but the fact that she hadn't done so yet implied something inside her had impeded her awakening.

Had dying and becoming a Vampire Queen flipped some sort of switch? No...

In the end, this was all groundless speculation. Maybe the only thing that mattered was that her efforts were rewarded.

And I should be content knowing my minion has obtained this mysterious power.

"The fish pie's ready!" Elfiné walked in, carrying a freshly baked pie right out of the oven.

It was a salmon pie, with mushrooms, cheese, and cream sauce. It looked crispy, and its crust had an appetizing golden-brown color.

"You made this, Miss Elfiné?" Leonis asked.

"Yes, pies are my specialty." Elfiné answered the boy's question quite confidently.

"It looks great! Let's eat it while it's hot," Riselia said, taking a seat in the chair to Leonis's right. Elfiné sat down on the boy's left.

...?!

Stuck between the two of them, the Undead King felt flustered; his face reddened. A pair of sizable bosoms flanked him on either side.

"Does being stuck in a sandwich feel good, boy?" Regina caught him blushing. She whispered the words playfully in his ear.

"Wh-what?! N-no...!"

"Oh, would you like a sandwich?" Riselia asked, reaching for an egg sandwich sitting on the table.

"Oh, no, Lady Selia, this boy here is feasting on an entirely different kind of sandwi—"

"Yes! I'd certainly like some of that pie!" Leonis exclaimed loudly, almost shouting in his panic.

"Here you are." Elfiné put a slice on his plate.

The pie's texture made a satisfying crunching sound as he cut into it, and warm sauce poured over his plate.

"Does the Assault Garden get fresh vegetables and fish?"

"Outside the residential areas, there are cultivation lakes and plants for producing different kinds of food. It's small, but our eighteenth platoon has our own vegetable garden there," Riselia answered.

...They cultivate fish inside the city?

Mankind's technological advancements in this area never ceased to amaze. Leonis bit into the pie. The savory taste of the sauce filled his mouth.

"...I-it's good!" Without thinking, Leonis had spoken with his natural voice.

The crunchy texture of the confection was exquisite, and the sauce's saltiness was just right.

"Heh-heh, thank you. Feel free to help yourself to more."

"It's great!" Regina exclaimed.

"Oh, I can't match your cooking, Regina." Elfiné shook her head humbly.

That left Leonis surprised. That maid could cook something better than this? Leonis had a maid of his own in Shary, but she was completely incapable of cooking.

...She's an accomplished assassin, though, so she's adept at handling poisons.

"So, Miss Riselia, think of an inscription for your Holy Sword yet?" Sakuya asked, half-busy helping herself to a piece of pie.

"Hmm, I haven't decided yet."

"An inscription?" Leonis asked.

"Yes—in other words, a name. It's necessary for registering a Holy Sword at the academy," explained Riselia.

"What about Slasher Cut Blade?"

"No, go for Shining Saint Sword!"

Sakuya and Regina didn't hesitate to offer their own suggestions. Riselia smiled wryly.

"...What do you think would be good, Leo?" Curious, she posed the question to Leonis.

"Hmm..."

He applauded his minion for her devotion, but this was a difficult question for him. Giving the Holy Sword an odd name would reflect poorly on him as her master. Leonis pondered for a moment...

"I can't really come up with anything when her Holy Sword's power isn't clear yet..." He came up with an innocuous response.

"...You're right. For now, it's just a very sharp sword, but it might have some special powers. I should have it registered once I'm more accustomed to using it." Riselia placed a hand over her chest.

"Speaking of registration, you still need to be registered, Leo...," Elfiné said.

"...Me?"

"We need to have your physical information scanned. My Holy Sword can do that and register it in the network. It'll be over in a jiffy, so could you stop by my room?"

"All right."

"That reminds me, where's he gonna stay?" Sakuya asked.

"I don't think there are any free rooms in the girls' Witch dorm."

"Oh, then how about you bunk with me, little guy? You'll have all the sweets you'll ever want."

"You can come to my room. I'm usually out the whole day."

"You're welcome in my room, too."

Regina, Sakuya, and Elfiné all chimed in with offers.

"...Y-you can't...!" Riselia got to her feet and waved her hands in protest.

"Lady Selia?"

"I'm Leo's guardian, so I'll take responsibility and take care of him." Riselia cleared her throat and gave Leonis a sidelong glance.

Leonis understood what she meant. Staying in the same room should help the two of them keep their respective secrets safe.

I do need to make sure she has a supply of mana...

"...I'd like to stay in Miss Selia's room," Leonis announced, grabbing hold of Riselia's sleeve.

...He had to admit Regina's offer of sweets was tempting, though.

"Are you sure that's a good idea, Lady Selia?" Regina asked.

"I am. My room always felt a bit too big for me."

"No, I mean, I'm concerned he might do something pervy to you."

"L-Leo would never...! Y-you wouldn't, right?"

"Of course not!"

Riselia's slightly anxious reaction evoked an astonished response from Leonis.

...If anything, Riselia struck him as a bit too naive. To an awkward degree.

"Regina, Leo is a ten-year-old boy. There's nothing to worry about."

"I suppose, but..." Regina eyed Leonis suspiciously. "I'm just gonna warn you now, kid. Lady Selia tosses and turns in her sleep, so be careful if you end up sharing a bed." The maid whispered the words in his ear.

"Regina, what are you telling him?!"

"You always hug my body like a big pillow, Lady Selia!"

"...Th-that's your fault for being so squishy, soft, and easy to hug!" the silver-haired girl stuttered, her face a deep red as she averted her gaze.

...It probably went without saying what part of her was so squishy and soft.

With Leonis's lodgings decided, the topic among the welcoming party shifted to more idle chatter. They talked about a new store that had opened in the commercial district, about the pet Sakuya kept in her room... Honestly, Leonis couldn't keep up with half of what they were saying. But for the first time in a thousand years, he had a chance to relax.

♦

Leonis's welcome party came to a close before it had grown too late in the evening. Afterward, Leonis was called into Elfiné's room so she could register his biological information using her Holy Sword.

...It truly was a boisterous meal, though, Leonis thought as he sat on Elfiné's sofa. Having three girls together was a...loud affair, to be sure, but such an energetic party would never have happened when Leonis was the Undead King. The only things that served as his company back then were darkness and silence. But...

A meal like that isn't so bad every now and then. Leonis shrugged.

He couldn't deny a part of him enjoyed spending his time that way.

Leonis looked around Elfiné's room. It was about as wide as Riselia's, but the fixtures and furniture left a more sophisticated impression. Between that and the wood-colored wallpaper, the place had a very mature feel.

His eyes came to rest on a framed picture sitting on top of a shelf. Riselia and the other members of the eighteenth platoon were absent. Instead, it was a different group. Perhaps Elfiné had belonged to a different platoon first.

...Doesn't seem like she would keep a picture if they'd fought and had a falling out, though.

It was hard to imagine that happening, given Elfiné's personality.

"Sorry to keep you waiting. I'm ready to start."

Elfiné returned from another room, carrying large tablet devices in both hands, and sat on a wheeled chair. She leaned forward to meet Leonis eye to eye.

"You can sit back and relax," Elfiné instructed.

"...O-okay."

"What's wrong? There's no need to be nervous." Elfiné smiled and tilted her head.

".........."

The girl's large breasts were level with Leonis's line of sight... True, she wasn't a match for the maid girl, but they were still more than enough to capture one's attention. Leonis turned away, a hint of red on his cheeks.

"All right, take off your clothes," she ordered.

"...Huh?" Leonis asked, unconsciously.

"Just your top will do. It's hard to read biological information through fabric."

".........."

"Sorry. I guess this is embarrassing for boys, too?"

"No, it's...it's fine."

Leonis removed his shirt.

"Oh, could you take off your undershirt, too?"

"Okay..."

He undid his buttons and took off his undershirt, revealing his unblemished white skin.

"Yeah, this will do. What lovely skin you have," Elfiné said, reaching her hands around his back. Her cold fingertips gently caressed his shoulder blades.

...Aaah... What is this...this sensation...?

Something about the feeling of an older girl's eyes on him filled his heart with intense bashfulness.

"Holy Sword—Eye of the Witch, Activate," whispered Elfiné, and transparent orbs appeared around her. What looked like numbers made of light began circling the orbs rapidly.

"All right, I'll register your data, Leo."

Elfiné placed a hand on Leonis's skin and closed her eyes, and as if in response, the orbs began circling him.

"...Hmm. This is kind of a strange pattern."

There was curiosity in Elfiné's voice.

"R-really?" The boy's heartbeat quickened.

"Yes. I can't see the flow of your mana..."

...*Damn. My mana obfuscation might be working too well...*

"Erm, Miss Elfiné, can I ask you something?" Leonis hurriedly tried to change the subject.

"Of course. What is it?"

"Why did you join this platoon?"

Riselia was a borderline dropout who hadn't been able to summon a Holy Sword. Leonis was genuinely curious as to why an upperclassman like Elfiné would join her team.

And then there's the photo...

The question prompted Elfiné to hang her head for a moment before she whispered her reply.

"...I lost the power of my Holy Sword."

"...Huh?" Leonis let slip without thinking. "What do you mean by that...?"

"This isn't the Eye of the Witch's true power." Elfiné shook her head. "It's only a limited ability."

"Really?"

"Yes. I used to be an attacker focused on high firepower instead of an operator."

"H-high firepower...?"

Leonis couldn't believe that was true of such a nice, level-headed, mature girl. Elfiné walked over to the picture and picked it up.

"The seventh platoon, the one I used to be a part of, was a skilled, well-balanced team. We were pretty high in the academy rankings, and we even went on Void subjugation missions. But then..."

She paused, taking a deep breath.

"Six months ago, my platoon was attacked by Voids during a ruin investigation."

"........."

She explained that a cunning pack of Voids had been waiting in the ruin. Elfiné's group was caught in a trap, and by the time they noticed, it was too late. Soon after they encountered the enemy, the Voids began radiating a powerful signal that jammed the platoon's communications and threw the chain of command into chaos. The Voids took the lives of two of the members of the squad...

Elfiné surviving was nothing more than a lucky coincidence.

No one had blamed her for abandoning her comrades and fleeing. Surviving and bringing data on the Voids back to Excalibur Academy was a Holy Swordsman's mission, after all.

Even so, she couldn't help but blame herself. Surviving filled her with guilt, and she kept torturing herself over it.

And so her Holy Sword lost its original power.

Elfiné's fingers shivered as they traced along Leonis's back. Each of the orbs hanging in the air illuminated faint light as if expressing her emotions...

"It was when I was in that sorry state that Riselia found me."

Riselia visited Elfiné time and time again after she'd shut herself in her room, imploring her to join her platoon.

"At first, I kept saying no. But she was so earnest, I eventually gave in. See...?"

"...Yes, I see."

It made sense to Leonis. Riselia did seem to have an odd power that allowed her to get her way in those kinds of situations. Perhaps it was charm...a charisma of sorts.

Elfiné took her hands off Leonis's back. The light emitted by the hovering spheres changed to a subdued shade of green.

"All right, I finished registering your biological information. I'll sync it up with the terminal."

She got to her feet and started rapidly entering information into a tablet.

"...Okay, so, 'Has a cute face but seems surprisingly preoccupied with breasts'... I... I see..." Elfiné turned to look at the boy with a mixed expression.

...Wait. What kind of data is this?!

"D-does biological data include that kind of thing, too?"

"Being a perv is bad, Leo."

"Y-you misunderstand...!"

Elfiné scolded him, and Leonis protested. Then, the boy's gaze suddenly fell on the screen of the other terminal sitting on the table.

It displayed a map of the area around Excalibur Academy. He did recall her mentioning that she was investigating the waters around these parts for a Void hive.

"Miss Elfiné, would it be all right if I took a look at that information later?"

"...? Sure, I don't mind..." The young woman cocked her head to one side at his request.

◆

Leonis returned to his room with a spare tablet that Elfiné had lent him. Apparently, she had several of them handy.

...Is she some sort of collector?

He opened the door to his room. As he entered, he could hear the inviting sound of water running from deeper inside... Riselia seemed to be taking a shower. Leonis gave a dry, loud cough and sat on his bed. As his fingers approached the tablet, he ran mana through it. The screen lit up, and a map dotted with red spots surfaced on the screen. It was data on Void locations over the last few months.

There really is a correlation...

Ogre, troll, chimera, wyvern... Those were all the names of monsters the Dark Lords' Armies employed in their war against humanity. The Voids Leonis saw had the characteristics of some of those ancient beasts. And larger Voids seemed to appear predominantly around ancient ruins and battlefields.

Among all the locations, more Voids appeared to originate from somewhere below the seas where the Seventh Assault Garden now sat. This was where the Wasteland of Sidon once stood. The site of a battle between the Dark Lords' Armies and the Six Heroes. The final resting places of countless monsters and undead, as well as the Archsage of the Six Heroes, Arakael Degradios, who had fused with the Holy Tree...

...Are Voids monsters of the past that have been transfigured by some sort of power?

He believed this theory to be sound. But even if that was the case, it still begged more questions. The remains of those ancient monsters should have disappeared long ago...

...And the Voids that took over the ruins disappeared after some time, too.

The cadavers of the Voids that Leonis had stored in his shadow had curiously vanished without a trace. Were the Voids invaders from another world or some type of weapon? But if they were weapons, they were a bit too diverse. Their reason for attacking mankind was still a complete mystery, as well.

...I may have to investigate this undersea nest of theirs.

These Voids could prove to be a great obstacle to the return of the Dark Lords' Armies. And as the Undead King, having these entities running rampant through his territory was irksome.

Suddenly sensing a presence, Leonis shut off the tablet's screen. The shadow at his feet wavered slightly.

"—I have returned, my lord."

The umbral maid, Shary Shadow Assassin, silently appeared in the room. The black-haired girl twirled in place and bowed elegantly.

"Oh, Shary. Good work," Leonis told her gratefully.

"Your words are wasted on me, my lord."

"So did you gather any information pertaining to the current state of mankind?"

"Yes..."

Shary presented Leonis with a large paper bag.

"What might this be?" the Undead King asked suspiciously.

"These are sweets, my lord. I believe they are called doughnuts."

"Hmm?"

Shary opened the bag, and a sweet scent wafted through the room.

"Have one."

"........."

Leonis took a doughnut out of the bag and bit into it.

"...How is it?"

"It's good."

The sweetness of sugar filled his mouth. It was a taste that made him crave some tea.

"I've brought you something to drink, as well."

"That's considerate of you."

"It's called tapioca juice."

It had an odd texture. Shary also began munching on a doughnut.

...That's fine, but don't spill your crumbs into my Realm of Shadow, if you please.

"I've brought all sorts of other delicacies as well. Like this stretching ice cream..." Shary started taking an assortment of sweets out of her paper bag.

"Wait, wait..."

"...?"

"That's enough about food. Don't you have any other data to share with me?"

"........."

"Don't tell me you spent all this time playing outside."

"........."

The umbral maid looked away, unable to meet her master's eyes.

"Well, that's fine... I suppose even their cuisine is a good indicator of mankind's current cultural level." Leonis sighed.

"I did gather some information, however." Shary cleared her throat. "There is no one in this city who seems to know about the Dark Lords..."

"Hmm, I assumed as much..."

According to Shary's intelligence, the citizens of this city were apparently unfamiliar with the gods of old or the war between the Dark Lords and the Six Heroes one thousand years ago. The fact that no one knew about such a great war was quite jarring, to say the least.

It's as if someone's wiped the past from the face of history...

Leonis decided he would go to Excalibur Academy's library tomorrow to look into it on his own.

"...Understood. Continue your investigation."

"Yes, my lord."

Shary nodded and...suddenly turned in the direction of the sound of running water in the bathroom.

"I see you've made that girl your minion."

"I did," Leonis confirmed.

"Ah. So you indiscriminately make everyone you come across into your minion, my lord," Shary said, pouting.

"What are you getting angry over?"

"I don't know what you're talking about. You're a dummy, my lord..."

"How can you call your master a 'dummy'? Now, listen and be amazed..."

"...What is it?"

"That girl, she's a Vampire Queen. The highest rank an undead minion can achieve. And she's recently awakened the mysterious power of a Holy Sword. Should I raise her properly, she will be a great confidant for the newly re-formed Dark Lords' Armies." Leonis gave a boastful smirk, as if to say, "How do you like *that*?!" Shary, however, merely scowled in further displeasure.

"A confidant... I see."

"Are you still upset over something?"

"Not at all. I hate you, my lord!" Miffed, Shary turned away from him and returned to his shadow.

"...What's her problem? I never could understand what that girl was thinking."

Leonis heaved an exasperated sigh and rolled onto the bed. He stared, unblinking, at the ceiling.

...Still, this world really has changed.

He was suddenly overcome with loneliness, as if there were a hole in his heart. Had *she* really reincarnated in this new era? Would he truly be able to rebuild the Dark Lords' Armies in this world devoid of demons and monsters...?

...No, a Dark Lord like myself can't afford to be so timid. Leonis smiled wryly.

He would have to seek her out. And if that meant hiding in this form, then that's what he would do.

Besides, this isn't all bad...

It may have been accidental, but he'd obtained a powerful vampire minion. She may have been inexperienced, but Riselia showed promise. With the Undead King's guidance, she'd surely become a promising retainer to him.

That's when he heard the bathroom door click open.

"...?!"

Reflexively, the Dark Lord turned his gaze toward the door. Gorgeous silver hair came into view... Riselia, dripping with water, emerged with a bath towel wrapped around her body.

"Oh, Leo. You can use the bath now, if you want."

...See, you're too naive!

Once again, she treated him like a child. Leonis was at his wit's end.

◆

On that same day, in the early morning...

Something awakened on the seafloor directly below the Seventh Assault Garden. It was one of the Six Heroes, the one praised for being the wisest of all mankind. The one who, long ago, had cast aside his human form to fuse with the Holy Tree.

It was the Archsage, Arakael Degradios.

But his form had long since changed from what it once was, becoming a massive seedbed producing denizens of nothingness—Voids...

However. A small fraction of the man once called the Archsage still remained within this new form, and it sensed the revival of his sworn nemesis.

...Undead... K...ing.. Unnnndeaaaaad...Kiiiiiiiiinnng...

Ancient hatred awakened a soul festering in emptiness. The roots of the Holy Tree writhed eerily below the water. Countless Voids birthed themselves from knots in its trunk.

Oooooooooooooooooooooooooooooooooh!

The flock of Voids raised their voices in celebration, unknown to those above. They cheered as one would to praise the return of a king...

♦

"Number 03 reporting. Large-scale change in the crust of the seafloor detected..."

"Roger, thirteenth platoon. Proceed with your survey, but be careful."

"Roger that— Hold on. What's that...?"

A research team of Holy Swordsmen, diving underwater with the power of a water-type Holy Sword, raised their voices in alarm.

"Number 03, what's wrong?!"

"Wh-what the...what the hell is that...? Aaah, aaaa-aaaaaaaah!"

The sight before the man's eyes struck fear into his soul.

"Calm down, Number 03. Please respond..."

"Are those...? Are those all Voids...?!"

The man's terrified voice vanished in a wave of static.

CHAPTER 7

THE PLACE I WISH TO PROTECT

He dreamed. He had long since forgotten that people dream in their slumber, because ever since he'd cast aside his human body, he hadn't had any dreams.

It was a dream of the time when he was still only a boy. The Hero of the Holy Sword, Leonis Shealto, was betrayed by the nobles of his kingdom and assassinated. It really was a surprisingly trite, commonplace story.

He cared little for the motive. Grudge, envy, hatred, vanity, fear... perhaps all those rolled into one. But the ten-year-old boy who had saved the world time and again was delivered to an unnatural death.

Even as he lay in the rain with a puddle of blood pooling beneath him, the boy didn't resent mankind... He'd seen plenty of its ugly sides, and many of its noble aspects as well. Even those who'd ordered his death weren't villains through and through.

"—Boy. Do you think this world is just?"

"...I don't care anymore."

The boy answered in a tired whisper; the woman simply extended her hand toward him.

"I wish to rebel against this world. What do you intend to do?"

And as she said those words with a smile, her expression was so...beautiful...

◆

...It's been a long time since I've dreamed about her.

It was a vivid dream that stirred memories of his past. Roselia—the girl known as the Goddess of Rebellion. She resurrected the boy once called a hero, changing him into a Dark Lord. She saved Leonis when he'd lost faith in this world, and then she went on to try to save the world itself. Shouldering that heavy burden with that small body of hers...

Plagued with a dull headache, he held his head as he sat up. Pajamas clung to his ten-year-old limbs. He still felt a bit numb.

"Nn... Nnnghh..."

And then an oddly sensual voice tickled his ears.

"...?!" He looked down in a panic.

Riselia turned over on the bed, sleeping pleasantly. Her breath leaked from between her lips. Her sleeping gown had become partially undone, exposing her chest. It rose and fell with each breath. Her silver hair glittered in the faint sunlight that crept in through the windows.

Wh-what is she doing here...?!

Leonis thought back on how he'd retired the night before. There was only one bed in the room, so Leonis had decided to sleep on the sofa. When he was the Undead King, he'd always slept in a stone coffin, so he wasn't very picky when it came to his bedding.

Yes, I definitely went to sleep on the sofa...

Leonis felt an unpleasant sensation on his neck. It was a bit swollen.

She didn't, did she...?

As Riselia cooed in her sleep, Leonis pinched her cheek.

"...Mmm, nnng..."

She only furrowed her brow in irritation but made no sign of waking up.

Leonis shrugged and whispered into her ear.

"Awaken, my minion..."

"...Aaaah?!"

The girl's eyes snapped open in surprise. He'd charged those words with mana to wake his subordinate.

"Good morning, Selia."

"G-good morning, Leo..." She looked at him, rubbing her eyes.

The sheets were pushed to one side, giving him a clear glimpse of her white panties. Leonis did his best not to look.

"Erm, wasn't I sleeping on the sofa?"

"Yes, I moved you to the bed. You'd catch a cold if you slept there."

"I'd probably be fine..."

Dark Lords catching colds was unheard of.

Though maybe it's possible in this body...?

It hardly mattered right now.

Leonis cleared his throat and glared at her with one eye half-open.

"You sucked my blood while I was sleeping, didn't you?"

".........."

Riselia looked away in a random direction.

"I have bite marks on my neck." He pressed harder to make her admit her guilt.

"J-just a bit...," she stammered, putting her index finger and thumb close together in the approximate shape of "just a bit." "It was late, and I couldn't help it... It just kind of happened..."

Vampiric impulses became stronger at nighttime, and having only just become a Vampire Queen, Riselia still had problems suppressing the urge.

"Don't misunderstand. It's not that I mind sharing my blood with a minion of mine, but at least ask me next time."

"...A-all right, I will. I'm sorry."

Still, to think she snuck up on the Undead King while he slept and sucked his blood. This Vampire Queen, he'd found, wasn't one to be trifled with.

"Also, no more sleeping in the same bed."

"Oh, Leo, are you at the age where that bothers you now?"

"I certainly am, yes." Leonis got up and started changing from his pajamas into his uniform.

"Where are you off to?" Riselia asked.

"The academy's library. I should be allowed inside now that I have a card, right?"

He planned to spend the day shutting himself away in Excalibur Academy's library like a recluse, looking into this era's history. Human society and its development, the appearance of the Voids, the power of the Holy Swords... There was plenty to research.

Besides, according to Shary's report, the old gods, Dark Lords, and Six Heroes weren't even legends in this age. Maybe studying history books would help him discover something.

A bit flustered, Riselia called to him as he prepared to leave.

"Um, the training grounds are reserved for your training curriculum this morning."

"Curriculum?" Leonis asked suspiciously.

"At Excalibur Academy, we can pick our training curriculums freely."

"...Really, now."

In Leonis's eyes, leaving the structure of the training to the pupils was rather inefficient. But seeing as the powers of the Holy Swords residing in each and every student were varied and wide-ranging, a comprehensive, uniform training curriculum wouldn't work, either. That aside...

"This is the first I've heard about reserving the training grounds."

"I put a curriculum together for you, Leo. As part of my privileges as your guardian," Riselia said nonchalantly. "I made sure you're training at the same time as me."

"Why did you do that?" Leonis asked, taken aback.

"You promised you'd train with me, right?"

"...Hmm." He had promised something like that. "Fine." Leonis shrugged.

◆

The Excalibur Academy training area Riselia reserved for them was an indoor space. The expansive, circular room had a domed shape.

"I reserved this gym for just the two of us, so we should be fine," Riselia said, stretching happily.

She was probably excited to be able to train as a Holy Swordswoman for the first time.

Leonis understood how she felt, at the very least.

"How about you show me your current strength, for starters?" Leonis suggested, tapping the bottom of his staff against the ground. "After that, we'll think about the details of your training."

"All right. Should we use a Void Simulator?" Riselia asked.

"No, I have a more realistic enemy for you," Leonis replied and began chanting a spell.

"—Valiant dead soldiers, obey the Undead King's call."

Leonis's shadow expanded in a circular manner and began writhing wildly. With the sound of frenzied rattling, dozens of incarnations of bone rose from the shadow.

"Wh-what? Are those...skeletons...?" whispered Riselia with a hint of fear.

...My word. So the youths of this age haven't even seen a skeleton before.

Skeletons would rise naturally in places filled with the miasma of death and were low-ranking monsters that had served as the core of the Undead King's army. Incidentally, Leonis could summon an army of hundreds of them at once.

"They're my lowest-ranking minions. Feel free to crush them."

"...Okay. Understood." Riselia nodded and held up her right hand into the empty air. "Activate!"

The next moment, her unnamed Holy Sword manifested in her hand. The embodiment of her soul. The elegant sword that defeated Muselle during the Holy Sword Trial.

"Then allow me..." Riselia's hair glowed with a silvery mana-filled light.

She swung her Holy Sword, crushing the skeleton solders to dust. The desiccated warriors continued their attack without pause, but Riselia mowed through them, annihilating the monsters.

...I'd expect nothing less of a Vampire Queen.

The skeletons were indeed undead, just like Riselia, but they were minions of the lowest rank, no match for a Vampire Queen. Despite the ease with which she moved, Riselia still wasn't capable of controlling the massive reserves of mana slumbering in her body. She was simply swinging her Holy Sword around with her vampire's enhanced brute strength.

...No, saying she's only swinging her sword around would be inaccurate.

Her swordsmanship wasn't bad. The girl's form was practical and made for true battle. Before long, she'd defeated all the skeleton soldiers.

"*...Huff, huff,* how did I do...?"

"Wonderful. Your skill with a sword is impressive." Leonis applauded.

"You know about swordsmanship...?" Riselia tilted her head questioningly.

Perhaps Leonis didn't look like the type to wield a blade.

"Well, a bit..." Leonis shrugged as if to avoid the question. "Did someone teach you, Selia?"

"Yes, my father had a blade-type Holy Sword."

...I see, her skill was passed down by her father.

"...I'm no match for Sakuya, though." Selia shook her head.

"A Vampire Queen's true power lies in her massive reserves of mana. Once you can control it, I'll teach you some sorcery."

"Really?"

"Yes. I think that would be for the best."

If she could use mana to reinforce her body, she'd be able to fight as a spellsword.

"Let's up the ante a bit, then."

He chanted a spell to summon skeleton beasts. These were skeletons formed from the bones of black wolves.

"These are beast-type undead that make use of group tactics. They won't be as easy as your first opponents."

"Okay!"

She wiped away her sweat and gripped her Holy Sword tight with both hands. She looked positively ecstatic just to be wielding the weapon.

Two hours later, their exercises were finished. The training grounds were littered with too many bones to count.

"Haah, haah, haah..."

Riselia was breathing heavily, her shoulders rising and falling.

"This seems like a good place to stop..."

Leonis expanded his shadow, retrieving the bones and returning them to his Realm of Shadows. This wasn't an age where bones were scattered across battlefields. If he retrieved any bones left around and poured his mana into them, he could use them again.

"...Thank you very much!" Riselia bowed her head.

Watching his minion grow certainly could be enjoyable.

"Do you need me to replenish your mana?"

"Ah... N-no, I'm fine...," Riselia stuttered, cheeks tinged with pink, after a moment of thought.

"All right. Then I'll be off..."

"Oh, Leo." The silver-haired girl stopped him before he could make for the library. "I'll be going out to the commercial district; could you join me?"

"No, I still need to..."

"I'll treat you to lunch. It'll be tasty."

".........."

The Dark Lord's stomach gave a thunderous growl.

...Damn this body! How incorrigible.

He'd planned to spend his day in the library, but it wasn't like the building was going anywhere. Checking out the city wasn't a bad idea.

...I shouldn't leave all the town investigation to Shary, I guess.

...And admittedly, the sweets she'd brought him the day before had piqued his interest.

♦

"That's strange," Elfiné whispered, squinting at the analysis screen.

"What's wrong, Miss Elfiné?" Sakuya peered at the screen from behind her back.

"The thirteenth platoon was investigating the seabed, but they haven't returned yet."

"The thirteenth platoon? Aren't they all skilled elites?"

"Looks like the academy's top brass hasn't publicized this yet."

The only ones who could access information withheld by the administration bureau were those who had Holy Swords like Elfiné's, capable of interfering with the information network. The academy was, of course, apprised of her Holy Sword's ability, but they were unaware she could access the network that deeply.

"Wait. Wait just a second...!" Elfiné exclaimed, eyes fixed on the screen.

"Mm?"

"This strange waveform... No, it can't be...!" She went pale.

She hoped this was a malfunction, but she'd seen this scenario countless times in the simulator.

"I have to report this to the bureau as soon as possible."

The moment she got to her feet, though, the screen filled with an explosion of red dots.

◆

"Here we are."

Riselia had driven the two of them on her vehicle to an area a short distance from the commercial district. It was a place with very little traffic, and there were no Excalibur Academy students in sight.

"Is this some kind of restaurant?" Leonis looked up at the building Riselia had pulled over next to.

"Yes, it's a restaurant that doubles as an orphanage. They shelter refugee children who have nowhere to go."

"An orphanage..." Leonis frowned.

He didn't have good memories of orphanages. It felt like a wound he'd forgotten about had opened again.

"What's wrong?"

"It's nothing."

It was a brick building, unusual for the Assault Garden. Riselia got off the vehicle, picking up a large box with both hands.

"Heave...ho..."

It looked heavy.

"If you used the mana afforded to you as a vampire, you'd be able to carry that pretty easily," Leonis advised her.

"I want to feel human in my normal, everyday life. Besides, any mana I use up, I'll need to have replenished, so..."

"...I understand," Leonis acknowledged, but he cast a spell to make the box lighter anyway.

A bell chimed as they entered the building, and...

"It's Selia!" "Seliaaaa!" "Selia's here!"

Several children ran into the room, hugging Riselia by the waist and legs.

...*How dare they cling to my minion like that...!* Leonis reflexively tensed but then reconsidered. *Well, they're only children. I shall overlook it this time.*

Forgetting he was a ten-year-old boy, too, he decided to forgive them.

...Leonis Death Magnus had always been the most tolerant of the Dark Lords.

Still, he had to wonder. Riselia was quite beloved by these children. She smiled wryly as she carried her package to the table, the kids still clinging to her.

"You haven't come to play for so long, Selia. We missed you!"

"I'm sorry. We had midterms at the academy, so I was busy..."

"Hyah!" A boy who looked to be five years old tried to flip up Riselia's skirt.

"H-hey, stop that!" she snapped, holding down the hem of her skirt.

...That was a little too hard to let slide. Even a forgiving Dark Lord couldn't help but be angered by this. But just as Leonis was about to cast a spell to trip the boy...

"Deen, what are you doing?!" The door to the kitchen opened, and an elderly woman stepped out. "I'm so sorry. You always help us out so much..."

"Not at all. I only hope I can actually be of some assistance around here..." Riselia turned to face Leonis and introduced him to the elderly woman. "This is Phrenia, the orphanage's owner."

"Who might this be?" the woman named Phrenia inquired.

"A boy I saved from a ruin. His name is Leo, and he's a Holy Swordsman."

"My, at such a young age?" Phrenia exclaimed.

"Cool!"

"Reaaaally?"

"Awesome!"

The children started gathering around Leonis.

"...D-desist!" commanded the Undead King, speaking in his natural voice. It had little success, as he soon found himself surrounded.

"Show us your Holy Sword!"

"What do you call it?!"

"S-stop, you can't do that..."

The oldest girl of the group (though only relatively so—she was just eight) tried to stop the other children, but they all started rustling Leonis's hair.

...I—I am a Dark Lord...!

"My, aren't you popular, Leo?" His minion made no attempt to rescue him, choosing to watch and giggle.

...I won't forget this, woman..., Leonis grumbled from the depths of his heart.

"I picked some veggies in the plant and brought them over."

Riselia opened the heavy box she'd carried in, revealing it was filled to the brim with produce.

She'd grown them herself in one of Excalibur Academy's plants.

"There isn't much, but they should taste good."

"Thank you. I'll make some soup." The old woman returned to the kitchen.

"I'll help her make lunch. Leo, you play with the kids until it's ready."

"What...?!"

Leonis reached out a hand, but Riselia disappeared into the kitchen.

"Show me your Holy Sword!" "What does it look like?!" "Your uniform is cool!"

"Ugh..."

With his ten-year-old limbs, he couldn't tear the kids off him, and using magic on children felt like it would hurt his dignity as the Undead King.

"S-stop it, you're bothering him...!" The oldest girl tried to reprimand the rest, but her frail voice didn't register.

Damn it all...! Leonis looked grudgingly at where Riselia had stood a moment ago.

♦

"It's ready."

Riselia peeked out of the kitchen fifteen minutes later, clad in an apron. In the blink of an eye, the children who had been playing with Leonis ran to the table.

...Good grief.

Leonis got to his feet, fixing his wrinkled clothes and ruffled hair. For the Undead King, who had once pushed back an army of tens of thousands of soldiers on his own, this was an unbelievable dishonor.

"E-erm... Are you...all right...?" The eldest girl among the children extended a clean handkerchief in a show of consideration.

"Mm, yes, those are just children playing around."

"I'm sorry... They didn't mean any harm, so..." The girl bowed her head several times in apology. "Oh, but I think it's really cool that you can use a Holy Sword, too!" Her face went red as soon as the words escaped her lips.

"Tessera, can you come here?"

"Y-yes!"

The girl bowed to Leonis and ran off.

"...Tessera, huh? It's good to see some kids are polite," Leonis muttered, combing his hair with his fingers.

The front of the orphanage was a public restaurant. A basket full of bread was sitting on the table alongside soup, salad, and deep-fried fish. The place wasn't very spacious, but it did have a pleasant atmosphere.

"I work here sometimes," Riselia said, taking off the apron.

Seeing her in an apron contrasted starkly with Leonis's perception of her noble heritage.

"On days when the restaurant is closed, everyone gathers here for meals."

Glancing outside, Leonis noticed the OPEN sign had been taken down.

...I see.

It had seemed she was well accustomed to handling kids, given how she'd taken care of Leonis while she thought he was one. It was likely because she was used to pitching in at the orphanage.

"You always help out so much, Miss Riselia," Phrenia said, bowing her head in thanks.

"Oh, not at all—you pay me a salary, after all..."

The children were seated at the table and already chewing away on bread. Leonis was just as hungry as they were but reached out calmly, demonstrating his dignity as the Undead King.

"How do you like the turnip soup?"

"...It's good." Leonis gave his honest opinion.

The homemade vegetable soup had a gentle saltiness to it, and its taste was simple but savory.

"Thank goodness. Regina taught me how to make it," Riselia said, giving a thumbs-up.

"Um...the bread tastes good, too." Tessera offered him a slice.

"Oh, thank you."

"Y-you're welcome..." Her cheeks turned rosy as Leonis accepted the food.

"All these children were rescued and brought from outside the city by Holy Swordsmen," Phrenia explained.

"That's right. They've all arrived here from different countries and places, seeking shelter."

"Selia, can we play later?"

"Sure. What do you want to play?"

The children embraced Riselia affectionately. She responded with a smile.

...*I see. This is the place she wants to protect,* Leonis thought as he watched her.

Her homeland was destroyed by the Voids, so she likely felt strongly about protecting children who'd suffered the same fate.

...*I'm a bit envious of her, I'll admit,* the Undead King thought. *The kingdom I am promised to protect is already long since lost...*

He thought back to the long ruined, nostalgic scenery of Necrozoa. But...

"C'mon, show me your Holy Sword!"

A chubby five-year-old boy tugged on Leonis's sleeve.

The child must have been truly courageous to accost the person of the Undead King.

"Phoca, the Holy Swordsman isn't a toy."

"Aww!" The boy whined at Phrenia's scolding.

"No, it's fine. I'll show them," Leonis offered generously.

Showing them a little something to distract them wouldn't be too bad. Making the children happy should please Riselia, too.

"What are you going to do, Leo?"

"...Hmm. Perhaps an artistic circus of skeletons would be good here."

"Skeletons?" "What're those?"

Curious questions from the kids came rapid-fire.

"M-maybe you shouldn't, Leo. You might scare them." Riselia tried to put him off the idea.

"...You think?"

"Yes. I mean, skeletons are a little scary..."

...Hmm. So skeletons are frightening.

Leonis actually found them quite cute.

"All right. Then how about some small, table-sized fireworks..."

But just as Leonis was about to chant a fire spell...

".........?!"

Brrrrrrrrrrrrrrrrrrrrrrrrrrrrrrrrrrrrrrrrrrrrrrrrrrrr!

A tremor shook the earth, causing the tableware to fall to the ground in a loud clatter.

"...Was that an earthquake?"

"No, that shouldn't be possible, the Assault Garden's fixed to the seabed by an anchor," Riselia replied.

Leonis's shoulders tensed.

And the next moment...the city's siren blared.

CHAPTER 8

STAMPEDE

With the shrill sound of the siren ringing in her ears, Instructor Diglassê rushed to Excalibur Academy's tactical conference room. Several other instructors were already gathered. The air was almost tangibly tense.

"What's the situation?"

"A contingent of Voids has appeared on the seabed directly beneath the Assault Garden," said the Holy Swordsman serving as acting commander-in-chief.

His name was Castoros Nekeo, a buff, muscular man in his late thirties.

"And it's not just any random large group. It looks like a Stampede..."

That word rendered everyone in the room speechless. A Stampede—a phenomenon where a swarm of Voids, led by a powerful leader called a Void Lord, ran amok. The memories of the Third Assault Garden's destruction at the hands of such a Stampede were still fresh in many peoples' minds.

"Were there no signs this was coming?" Diglassê asked as she broke into a cold sweat.

"Unfortunately, we don't have any means of detecting a Void Lord," one bespectacled researcher replied.

"Do we know how many Voids are out there?" asked a white-haired old man—he was a military advisor dispatched from Camelot.

"Their numbers are estimated to exceed several hundred..."

"Several hundred...?!"

That many enemies meant their chances were hopeless, even if they were all small Voids. But if this truly was a Stampede, then there was a possibility that a Void Lord, an extremely large class of Void that commanded the hordes, might appear.

"Whatever the case, our top priorities are evacuating the civilians and locating the commanding Void. Order the academy's defenses tightened while our platoons work on leading the civilians to safety."

◆

Riselia rushed outside, siren blaring all the while. Leonis followed her, not quite sure what was going on...

...*Wh-what's that?!*

The sky was covered in a sea of gray clouds. No, not clouds. A flock of deformed winged monsters flew across the horizon, their numbers blotting out the sun.

"Voids..."

These were smaller than the ones he'd seen in the ruin, but... there was no mistaking it. These were the same kind of creatures. The siren blared in his ears like a scream, and the citizens of the Assault Garden walking along the street simply looked up, shocked.

Where did all these flies come from...?

He recalled the underwater colony Elfiné was looking into...

"No! Why is there a Stampede here...?!" Riselia gaped with an expression of sheer despair.

"What's going on?"

"I don't know." She shook her head. "Anyway, we need to evacuate everyone..."

The moment she turned around to the orphanage, a thick, black mist suddenly filled the street. A massive shadow grew where the miasma was the thickest. It quickly took the form of a collection of deformed nightmares resembling many different beasts—Voids.

"Aaaaaaaaaaaaaaaaaaaaaaaaaaaah!"

Terrified screams erupted from all sides at the sight of the Voids. Some people ran, while others boarded vehicles and took off.

"Everyone, calm down! Head for the shelters!" Riselia called.

But her voice failed to reach the panicked people. The girl bit her lower lip bitterly, likely recalling the Stampede that had destroyed her hometown.

Four, five, six...chimera-like Voids slunk from the black fog, one after another.

"Do these Voids have a designation, too?"

"They're a large class of Void that's a mix of different beasts—we call them the manticore class."

...I see. So they call them manticores instead of chimeras.

But they were still based on the appearance of an ancient monster.

Voooooooooooooooooooooooooooooooooooooooooooooo!

The manticore-class Voids swung their tails around, smashing nearby buildings.

"...!"

Riselia looked back. The children were still in the orphanage. They wouldn't be able to escape in the chaos.

"We need to call the academy for help..."

Riselia activated the communication earring dangling from her ear but heard only static.

"Leo, get behind me...," Riselia said.

She still didn't know Leonis had defeated the Voids in the ruins. She only knew of the bit of power he'd shown when they'd dueled Muselle. His minion stood in front of Leonis in an attempt to protect him. It wasn't that she was overly confident about the power of her Holy Sword. No. Leonis could see the intent in Riselia's eyes. It was the solemn resolve of a knight.

"Aren't you scared?"

"Of course. If I didn't have my Holy Sword, I might've run away. But..." Riselia looked straight ahead. "I can't afford to run anymore!"

One of the manticore-class Voids crushed the ground beneath its feet as it leapt up. The creature's body arced through the air, closing the distance between itself and the two of them in a single bound.

Zoooooooooooooooooooooo!

Its massive bulk gouged the asphalt beneath it, forming small craters as it landed.

"Activate!" Riselia cried, and a slender sword formed in her hands. "Haaaaah!"

She raised her voice in a battle cry and made a swift strike to the Void's head. Her sword flashed, but...

"...The blade isn't going through...?!"

Her attack did little more than scratch the monster's head, failing to inflict any fatal damage.

"*Gooooooooooooooooooooooooooh!*"

The large Void swiped with a foreleg at Riselia—

"Beruda Gira!"

Bang!

Leonis fired a Heavy Gravity Bombardment spell that distorted the ensorcelled air. The manticore-class Void's colossal frame was crushed under the pressure of his magic.

"I commend your courage, but assessing the enemy's strength is important," he said.

"L-Leo?!" Riselia took a step back, a shocked expression on her face.

The Staff of Sealed Sins, having emerged from Leonis's shadow, was clenched in the boy's hand.

"Was that you just now?"

"Be careful. There are still more coming...," Leonis said, alert.

The large flock blotting out the sky was descending. Amid the swarm was one that clearly dwarfed the rest.

"Is that...? Could that be a Void Lord?!" Riselia gave a nervous gasp.

In contrast, Leonis simply smirked indomitably.

...Oh, how very nostalgic!

◆

Between the piercing howls of the siren, the members of the eighteenth platoon ran through the third residential district, the most densely populated in the Garden.

"Please head to your nearest shelter!"

Elfiné used her Holy Sword's orbs to search the area. Most citizens had already evacuated to underground shelters, but there might've still been some who'd failed to escape in time. The sound of flapping wings could be heard in the distance.

"...Where did such a huge pack come from...?!" Regina, who was stationed on higher ground, exclaimed as she used her Drag Howl to bombard the flying Voids.

The Assault Garden had already shifted to defense mode and

had been firing off great barrages of gunfire, but conventional weapons didn't affect their enemies. Many of the younger students had already fled. Even most among those who could summon Holy Swords, few had any real experience fighting Voids.

After all, this was the first Void attack on the Seventh Assault Garden in the six years since its construction.

"Miss Elfiné, can you get in touch with Lady Selia?"

"There's a powerful jamming signal interfering with the connection."

Apparently, one Void was somehow disrupting their long-distance communications.

"...Lady Selia..."

"I understand your concern, Regina, but right now we need to..."

"Yes, I know."

Regina was a survivor of the Third Assault Garden tragedy and Riselia's childhood friend...

To say she felt uneasy was an understatement.

And Leo's missing, too...

They were both likely at the orphanage near the commercial district. Elfiné had sent one of her orbs there to investigate.

The Voids' eyes shone crimson as their jaws creaked open with a hideous sound. They may not have had any intelligence per se, but Elfiné got a definite sense there was a kind of unity among the pack.

"There's too many of them...!"

"Handle the large Voids with groups of four or more!" The battalion commander's voice crackled from the communication terminal.

The commanding officer took over tactical command, but the actions of each individual platoon fell to their captains. That was because only the platoon's members were familiar with the powers of their Holy Swords and which tactics were most effective.

"Regina, I'll cut a way through. Cover me."

Sakuya stepped forward, her white Sakura Orchid garb fluttering in the wind. There wasn't a trace of fear in her eyes. At the bottom of those clear pools burned an intense hatred for Voids.

"Cut down all that opposes you, Blade of Lightning—Activate!"

Chanting the words that unlocked her power, the girl summoned her Holy Sword. The very soul of the Sakura Orchid clan materialized in her hand—a katana. It was her Holy Sword—the Blade of Lightning, Raikirimaru.

"Let's do this, you accursed creatures!"

Sakuya's boots kicked against the ground, the wind whistling as each stroke of her sword moved with incredible speed, as though she were a bolt streaking through the heavens. Blue electricity surged, licking at Voids and scorching them to embers. But the lightning was only a by-product of her power. With each slash, she accelerated, moving ever faster—such was the true strength of Sakuya's Holy Sword.

"Mikagami-style swordsmanship—Dance of the Sakura!"

A flash of Sakuya Sieglinde's sword, and cuts bloomed on her enemies like flowers in spring. This technique the small girl employed was a secret art passed down in her home village. A memento of the Sakura Orchid clan.

Carnage incarnate, she sliced through the smaller Voids.

"I've got your back, Sakuya!"

Regina's Drag Howl belched a gout of flame, blowing back a flock of predators.

That was when it happened.

"Hold up! There's something coming!"

Elfiné's exclamation ripped through her communication device. It was something only her Holy Sword—the Eye of the Witch—had detected.

"There's...something huge approaching...!"

Asphalt cracked and crumbled at the impending threat.

"Uooooo, uoooooooooooooooooooooooo!"

A massive Void the size of a five-story building appeared. A titanic beast with seven heads.

"It can't be... A hydra class...?!"

◆

Voids surrounded Riselia and Leonis as the two stood with their backs to the orphanage. Large manticore classes and small hell hound classes drew ever nearer. And behind them, the massive Void that filled the gray sky.

"...Is that the Void Lord?" Leonis asked.

"Yeah, that's probably the one leading the others..." Riselia nodded.

The way it flapped its wings was reminiscent of dragons, the tyrants of the skies. But its wings looked to have rotted from the dark miasma that had appeared with the Voids. The titanic Lord's body writhed in eerie patterns.

To think, even the great dragonkin have been reduced to Voids... Leonis felt an indescribable emotion prick at his heart.

They were once a proud race that reigned over the skies one thousand years ago. The Dragon Lord Veira had fought bravely during the war against the Six Heroes.

This is a show of mercy. The Undead King will put you to rest.

Leonis held up the Staff of Sealed Sins. If this Void possessed a resistance to magic on par with that of a dragon, a normal spell wouldn't be enough to down it.

"*Guuuuuuuoooooooooooooooooooooooooooooooooooh!*"

The towering Lord howled, and as if responding to its call, the Voids on the ground began swarming around Leonis.

"Selia, I'm going to use a powerful spell. I need you to protect me for a while."

"All right!" Riselia stepped forward, brandishing her Holy Sword.

As Leonis chanted a wide-range destructive spell, he also prepared a multitude of strengthening spells. Attribute Protection, Mana Barrier, Mana Augmentation, Physical Augmentation, Agility Augmentation...

"Haaaaaaaaaaaaaaaaaaaaah!"

Riselia lunged at the swarm. The tip of her blade caught the light as she cut freely through her enemies. Her movements were quick and fluid, proof her body was acclimating to fighting as a Vampire Queen.

"Celestial Stars in the Heaven, Ye Haughty Sealers of Judgment..."

Charging his staff with large amounts of mana, Leonis began chanting a tenth-order spell.

...My word, what am I even doing here...? Leonis thought with a hint of self-deprecation.

His objective was to find the reincarnation of the goddess and restore the Dark Lords' Armies. He shouldn't care whether a human city got destroyed by Voids or not. Him putting on such a large show of power here only ran the risk of exposing his identity. However...

Leonis glared at the massive Void. Any fool who would pick a fight with the Undead King and his minion couldn't be ignored. He completed his spell.

A tenth-order destruction spell—Dark Star Beckoning, Zemexis Jyura.

Countless fireballs were conjured from thin air, raining down on the Voids. The explosions shook the air around them, scattering waves of heat in all directions.

"...Ah, L-Leo? Isn't this dangerous?!" a somewhat panicked Riselia asked.

"This spell is set to follow its targets, so just stay put!"

"I can't hear— Aaaaah!"

Booooooooooooooooooooom!

The fireballs collided with nearby buildings, reducing them to rubble. Black smoke issued around them, and countless craters dotted the ground. A number of the manticore-class Voids had been blasted to bits in the barrage.

"Hmm. Perhaps I got the coordinates a bit off?" Leonis cocked his head with a displeased expression.

Controlling his mana really was too difficult with his current body. Regardless, Leonis felt confident he'd adjust to it soon enough.

The shock from the explosions had knocked some decorations from the roof of the building, but the orphanage was otherwise unharmed. And when the intermittent explosions died down...

"What was that...?" Riselia got to her feet.

"Be careful. *It's still alive.*"

"Huh?"

No sooner had Leonis's words left his lips, than...

"Guooooooooooooooooo!"

With a roar, the massive Void that had been knocked to the ground rose back up. The creature measured thirty meters long. Its massive form was suddenly enveloped with the faint light of a mana flare.

"Draconic Light Armor, huh? An innate spell."

Dragons that lived long enough acquired intelligence and were capable of using innate spellcasting unique to dragonkin. Judging by its size, this Void was likely an elder dragon.

So even without its intelligence, it can still use sorcery...

Leonis hadn't expected his spell to defeat it, of course. The Void Lord howled and raised its crooked neck. Its mouth filled with red-hot air...

"Selia, get down!"

Leonis reflexively deployed a mana barrier. The spherical shield blocked the dragon's blazing breath, while the flames lashed their surroundings. The asphalt melted, forming a sea of lava around them.

The Void Lord then started chanting a second spell, forming multiple magic circles in the air around it. A large-scale destructive spell that would eradicate their surroundings indiscriminately. At this rate, the orphanage would be caught in the destruction, too...

Will I be able to cancel it out with a spell of equal strength in time...?!

The limitations of the human body restricted how quickly Leonis could chant.

"...I won't let you!" Riselia made a fierce charge forward, Holy Sword in hand. "Hyaaaaaaaaaaaah!"

She slashed, her shining, silvery hair streaming through the air. Any normal Void would've been cleaved in two by the attack, but the dragon's scales deflected even the blade of a Holy Sword. The Void Lord lifted its tail and slammed it against the ground.

"...!"

She reflexively avoided the tail but was blown aside by its shock wave.

"Zamd! Zamd! Zamd!"

Leonis quickly undid the spell he was chanting and fired

several Cursed Burst Shots—a second-order spell. Though the technique was capable of crushing even boulders, the dragon barely staggered. The Void Lord began chanting the large-scale destruction spell again.

But then... A gigantic black wolf leaped from the shadow of the rubble and sank its fangs into the Void's neck.

"*Guoooooooooooooooooooooooooooooooooooooooooooooh!*"

"Blackas!"

It was indeed Leonis's comrade in arms, the prince of the Realm of Shadows—Blackas Shadow Prince.

The Void Lord thrashed its neck, struggling to shake off its attacker, but the great obsidian wolf refused to release its jaws. Leonis used that moment to invoke his spell.

"Perish, Lackwit King. Know Your Own Foolishness...!"

The spell was loosed, and Blackas took cover in the shadows. It was a tenth-order spell—Massive Extinction Malediction, Meld Gaiez.

An orb of nothingness appeared above the Void Lord, bearing down on the creature and crushing it into the earth.

"*Grrrrrrroooooooooooooooooooooooooooooooooh!*"

Cavernous fissures ran through the ground and split open. The Void's massive form disappeared into the bottom of the chasm. Leonis then fired several Madia Zolf spells—the Incandescent Inferno Cannon. With each blast, flames surged up from the depths of the abyss.

May you rest in peace, proud king of the dragons...

Among all monsters, Leonis was especially fond of dragons. He had always found their aloof strength and pride very relatable. Thus, seeing them reduced to these creatures was unforgivable in his eyes.

Darkness filled the bottomless chasm. There had likely been a vast trench beneath this city to begin with. Turning, Leonis found Riselia breathing heavily.

"Do you need some blood?"

"...I-I'm fine..." The girl looked away.

Then something suddenly erupted from the cracks in the ground.

"What?!"

They were writhing tree branches and roots. In the blink of an eye, they coiled around Riselia's body and dragged her down into the depths.

"Selia!"

"Leooooooo...!"

Leonis reached out to grab her, but his fingertips only grasped empty air. With a gentle sound, her earring communication device fell at Leonis's feet.

What in the world is this...?

The encroaching roots seemed to be devouring the remains of the Voids that littered the area, growing larger as they did.

It's eating the Voids?!

Leonis had seen this once before: a tree's roots multiplying without end and devouring the armies of the undead. He'd seen it one thousand years ago in the final battle of the Dark Lords' Armies...

"...Oh, I see. So it's you...," Leonis said, his lips forming the name of his hated nemesis. "One of the Six Heroes...Arakael Degradios!"

CHAPTER 9

THE FALLEN HERO

The Archsage of the Six Heroes—Arakael Degradios. His age already exceeded two hundred even before he achieved immortality by merging with the Holy Tree worshipped by the elves.

Once an old man lauded as the wisest and greatest of mankind, Arakael had lain waste to the Dark Lords' Armies on countless battlefronts. One thousand years later, the Archsage had appeared in battle yet again, but the form he took was a far cry from the one Leonis knew.

"A Void...?" Leonis found himself swallowing nervously upon seeing what his old rival had become.

The bark of the Holy Tree had festered, inflamed with the same black mist that had accompanied the Voids that attacked the Garden. Its branches, which once produced the fruit of immortality, were now adorned with the writhing faces of countless Voids. They raised their voices in unnatural roars as the creatures tried to crawl out into the world.

The Holy Tree was birthing Voids.

"...Now I understand. *You're* the Void Lord," Leonis concluded.

Voids were indeed ancient monsters; they'd been transfigured by some unknown power. Since that was the case, it wasn't a far leap to assume the Six Heroes had become Voids as well.

—LE...O...N...ISSSSSS...

The countless faces of the Voids mouthed his name as if chanting a curse. Arakael's hatred was palpable even a thousand years later. No, perhaps it was more appropriate to say his anger had been growing, boiling here for one thousand years...

"Did you truly long to meet me again that badly, you pathetic corpse?" Leonis cracked a thin smile.

He chanted a sixth-order spell, the Cursed Inferno Blast, Mel Ziora.

Booooooooooooooooooooooom!

The raging flames incinerated the Voids along with the writhing roots.

So it snatched Riselia away to lure me out...

—LEO...NISSSS...

"Just you wait," Leonis said, stepping over the charred remains of the Voids. "This time, there won't even be ashes left when I'm done with you."

He glanced back, feeling eyes on himself. The children of the orphanage were watching Leonis with frightened expressions.

...I suppose I can't blame them.

—It wasn't all that different from that day so many years ago.

He was used to seeing people look at him like that. Possessing such overwhelming power stirred fear in the hearts of men. That was true even when he'd saved the kingdom as a hero.

...As the Undead King, I should be pleased by this.

Leonis heaved a small sigh and walked away from the orphanage. All the Voids in the area were destroyed, and there was little danger of it being attacked again. It was just a matter of time until the academy's Holy Swordsmen arrived anyway.

Whether this orphanage was attacked or not didn't matter much to Leonis, but this place was dear to his minion's—to Riselia's—heart. Leonis held up his Staff of Sealed Sins and chanted.

"Eighth-order spell—Zoah Doma."

The Obsolescence Barrier settled over the orphanage like a black fog of death. With another spell, the Undead King conjured a pair of greater skeleton knights, powerful undead warriors. They were reliable enough to be trusted with the protection of great treasure or nobles. Leonis realized that the barrier he'd conjured was a bit wider than necessary, but it wouldn't be broken through easily.

"I put up a barrier. If you don't want to die, stay inside this building." Leonis addressed the frightened children with an indifferent tone.

He then made to leave, only to hear a voice call from behind.

"...Erm... P-please wait...!"

The orphanage's door opened, and the oldest girl among the children stepped out timidly. Tessera.

"L-Leo..."

A skeleton knight brandished its sword, ready to stop the girl, but Leonis raised a hand, prompting the knight to sheathe its weapon.

"E-erm..." The girl was so nervous, her voice couldn't pass her lips.

"What is it?"

"Th-thank you...for protecting us...," Tessera said, bowing her head.

"...Y-yeah..."

Those unexpected words of gratitude left him somewhat surprised.

"Please, save Selia." She'd likely seen Riselia's abduction. Her head remained bowed her head as she made the request.

"I will. Leave it to me." Leonis nodded, patting her lightly. "I promise I'll bring Selia back."

"O-okay!"

The skeleton knight pulled the girl back inside.

The Undead King always kept his promises.

His back to Tessera, he headed for the giant fissure in the ground. At the edge of the great shaft, sitting on top of a pile of rubble, was a black wolf.

"—Our old nemesis has returned from the grave, it seems."

"Blackas, what are you doing here?"

"I've hastened to your side, my friend, slaughtering the creatures in my path."

"Did you eat them?"

"I would not. They seem disgusting." Blackas shook his head and dropped a large cloth sack at Leonis's feet.

"What's this?"

"The spoils of war. I gathered them while investigating the city. They are far more delicious."

Inside the sack were several skewers lined with grilled meat.

"You didn't steal these, did you?"

"I'm a member of the royal family of the Realm of Shadows. I would never do such a thing," Blackas scoffed, disappointed. "I allowed the humans to stroke my tail, for which they gave me these."

"...I see."

He would have preferred Blackas not doing anything to make himself conspicuous.

"I am hungry, though. Would you share these with me?"

Leonis may have used one powerful spell too many. Using his dark magic the same way he had back when he was the Undead King was problematic in this body.

Blackas picked up one of the skewers in his mouth, presenting it to Leonis. The boy quickly scarfed down the grilled meat and threw the skewer into the pit. Riselia had likely been snatched away to bait Leonis, but the tree might've also been trying to assimilate the massive power of a Vampire Queen. If that was the case, he had to hurry.

"Now, then. It's about time you returned my minion, Archsage."

◆

"Thundering Lightning Slash!"

Raikirimaru's blade flashed through the air. Sakuya Sieglinde's transcendent, well-honed swordsmanship sent the heads of the hydra-class Void soaring into the air. Her movements struck as swiftly as her weapon's namesake. She bounded along the ground, moving faster and faster.

"Two-Stage Moonflower Flurry!"

The robes of her homeland danced in the wind as she once again severed one of the Void's heads.

"Not bad! So you're that young student they say is skilled enough to slay Voids?"

A Holy Swordswoman wielding a wind-type Holy Sword fought side by side with Sakuya. She was a vanguard attacker from the ninth platoon that had been dispatched to the same sector.

"If you keep flapping your tongue in the middle of battle, you'll die, ma'am," Sakuya remarked curtly.

"Yeah, yeah. I get it..."

The other girl didn't seem to take offense and moved to slash at the hydra class's legs.

"Its heads are already regenerating. Burn away the severed sections!"

Elfiné had been analyzing the Void's classification and relaying the data to all the other platoons using her tablet.

"Leave that to me! Drag Howl!"

Bang, bang, bang, bang!

Regina's Holy Sword spewed fire. Her attacks—capable of single-handedly defeating an ogre-class Void—sent ripples through the air as the hydra-class Void was enveloped in flames.

But when the dust and smoke cleared...

"N-no way...!" Regina ground her teeth bitterly.

The Void didn't seem to have taken any damage. Instead—there were tree roots growing out of the neck stumps left behind following Sakuya's attacks.

"Wh-what're those?!"

"...I don't know. There's no match for that kind of specimen in our data." Elfiné shook her head. This was different from a regular hydra class.

"...Spread out!" the ninth platoon's acting commander ordered, sensing incoming danger.

Three vanguard attackers finished their combo assault and jumped away. Sakuya refused the command, however. She simply stood in front of the Void, staring her enemy down.

Crrrrrrraaaaaaaaaaaaassssshhhhh!

The roots bursting out of the severed heads of the hydra class whipped about, destroying the nearby buildings.

"Sakuya?!" Elfiné raised her voice in a shout.

"How strange. You monsters become more and more like specters every day."

Dodging an attack by a hairbreadth, Sakuya tightened her grip on Raikirimaru. Those treelike necks moved as if without regard for the Void they were attached to. The commander shouted something, but Sakuya didn't hear it.

Sakuya had a tendency to be blinded to what was happening around her in the heat of battle. It was why no platoon had sought her out, despite her prowess.

But regardless of that...

...Thank goodness.

Elfiné heaved a sigh of relief knowing Sakuya was still alive. Had her Eye of the Witch been working at full strength, its overwhelming power would have allowed her to provide cover for all the attackers on the field at once. But the true power of her Holy Sword remained sealed from her.

...I'm still too afraid of Voids.

Elfiné hugged herself, as if trying to restrain a shiver running through her limbs. She couldn't conquer the terror she'd felt since that fateful day.

Even so, she chose to stay on the battlefield and offer intel to the Holy Swordsmen fighting on the front lines. That was the greatest contribution she could make right now.

"El...finé... Miss Elfiné..."

Elfiné suddenly jolted in surprise as a voice echoed in her mind.

"...Leo, is that you?!"

It was indeed the boy's voice.

"Good, you can hear me..."

One of the orbs she had sent to the nearby areas must have served as a relay. Leonis's voice came in clearly.

"Yes... Are you using Selia's communication device?"

Leonis shouldn't have been supplied with one of his own yet.

"Yes, this is Miss Selia's."

An unpleasant feeling slithered through Elfiné's thoughts. If the two of them were in the same place, why wasn't Riselia herself using the device?

"Miss Selia's been captured by Voids."

Elfiné's fear was right on the money.

"...?!"

She was at a loss for words.

The Voids abducted a human being? Why...?

But the next thing Leonis said only served to frighten her further.

"I'm going to rescue her. Miss Elfiné, I need you to use your ability to pinpoint her position."

"You're going to go save her...alone?"

Elfiné was shocked by his suggestion. It was too reckless. He may have had the power of a Holy Sword, but he was only a ten-year-old boy.

"—Yes."

"Just wait for a bit, I'll ask another platoon to help rescue her right now..."

"We won't make it in time if you do that," his cold voice said through the terminal. "And besides, you haven't the capacity to spare any capable fighters, do you?"

"That's..."

Elfiné returned her "eyes" to the battlefield. Sakuya's group was fighting to the best of their ability, but the massive Void was proving to be too much for their small numbers. They were struggling.

"I'll bring her back. Miss Elfiné, please tell me where she is."

"........."

I should stop him.

Going on a rescue mission on his own was insane. But there was no guarantee Riselia would survive until another platoon could come to help her.

Leonis fell into a short, hesitant silence.

"...Miss Elfiné, could you use your 'Eye' to look at the sector where I'm located?"

"...? I could, but..."

Dubious, she linked her vision with one of the orbs flying past. When she did...

"What is this...?" Words of astonishment left her lips.

Tree roots had destroyed the asphalt, carving scars into the ground. And...scattered all around Leonis were the remains of countless Voids.

"Did you kill all of...?"

"Yes, I did this," Leonis answered tersely. **"I'll tell you every-thing later, Miss Elfiné. For now, please just trust me."**

His voice was far too calm and collected for a ten-year-old.

"........."

Elfiné swallowed a quick breath.

"...All right. I'll try." She nodded.

After seeing that much, she had to believe. Cutting off all other information for a moment, she focused on tracking Riselia's registered information. The reception was weak. The miasma the Voids released was likely jamming it. And yet...

"...She's underground... Deep underground. Four layers below..."

The underground area of the Assault Garden was a concealed space kept hidden as a military secret. Its interior was sealed off by countless bulkheads, making it difficult even for Elfiné's Eye of the Witch to pierce. Shutting out her own senses, she focused as hard as she could.

"You should be able to access the main shaft from where you are, Leo. I'll use my Holy Sword to unlock the bulkheads, so you should be able to go as deep as the seventh stratum..."

"I'll destroy the bulkheads if need be. Lead me down the shortest route possible."

"Destroy them...? F-fine, all right..."

As soon as she had refocused herself to the task...

Booooooooooooooooooooooooom!

"...?!"

A catastrophic blast reverberated, shaking Elfiné's body.

"...Miss Elfiné, what's happening?"

Elfiné got to her feet and returned her senses to her immediate surroundings. The hydra-class Void had broken through the vanguards. It rushed forward, the earth trembling beneath its feet with every step.

"Wait, is it coming this way?! Miss Elfiné, look out...!" Regina shouted from the rooftop of a nearby building.

".........."

Elfiné couldn't move, though. The trauma of losing her old squadmates to a Void attack had left her frozen, chained where she stood.

"Ah..."

She cowered, shrinking in place, and squeezed her eyes shut. And then...

The air whistled as the Void was cleaved in two.

...Huh?

One of the heads of the Void bearing down on her had been, quite suddenly, removed from its body.

Fyoo! Fyoo! Fyoo!

The rest of its heads were lopped off as well, in quick succession. The hydra-class Void sank to the ground before Elfiné's eyes.

"...Wh-what?" Sakuya whispered in surprise, Raikirimaru still gripped in her hands.

"I don't...know..."

One of the orbs of Elfiné's Holy Sword then caught a glimpse of a small shadow standing on the rooftop of a nearby building. A girl clad in a maid's uniform retracted whips made of darkness into her hands.

"...Good grief. My Undead King certainly has a habit of working his maid to the bone," she whispered in slight displeasure before grumpily munching on a doughnut.

♦

"Farga!"

Boooooooooooom!

Leonis's Bursting Curse Shot tore through the bulkhead barriers as he continued his silent descent. He was heading down the massive shaft leading into the depths of the Assault Garden's underground. His drop was regulated by powerful gravity-control magic.

"I never imagined there'd be such a vast labyrinth beneath the city," Blackas remarked from Leonis's shadow.

"There are probably tunnels spread out for transporting supplies and manpower."

Perhaps they had been dug with the intent of moving Holy Swordsmen swiftly in case of emergency, but the buried passages were blocked by the roots of the tree.

"Still, mankind's magical technology has advanced so far," Leonis marveled as he burned through the roots attempting to devour the intruder.

Even the dwarves hadn't achieved a structure this large.

...Which reminds me, I haven't seen any elves or dwarves at this academy, Leonis thought.

Were they isolated from human society, or perhaps...?

Destroyed by the Voids...? I don't remember them being that weak.

The demi-human alliance had made a pact with mankind. The elves of the Spirit Forest in particular had given Leonis a hard time back in the day.

"...Keep going that way. The route continues straight ahead."

"Understood."

Following Elfiné's instructions through the earring, Leonis landed on a platform sticking out from the shaft's side.

"Farga!"

He destroyed the closed bulkhead barrier and advanced into the dark corridor with his staff in his hands lighting the way.

"...—Keep going...fighting...city's power source...—"

The static grew worse and worse. Perhaps the Void Lord was at fault for the interference, which must have meant they were getting close. The sound of Leonis's shoes clicking against the floor echoed loudly through the corridor.

"You sent Shary to help the humans?" the black wolf asked from within the boy's shadow.

"Mm, yes..."

Shary may have been a ditzy maid, but she was a skilled assassin. She was no match for Blackas in terms of sheer combat prowess but was still capable of toppling a castle all on her own.

"We're up against one of the Six Heroes. Are you sure not bringing her along was a good idea?"

"...The two of us will be more than enough," Leonis answered as if to evade the question.

He realized what Blackas was getting at, of course. Why did he send his right-hand woman, Shary, to protect the humans? His minion Riselia was another matter, but there was no rational reason he would elect to defend the other members of the eighteenth platoon.

Leonis cleared his throat, feeling Blackas's suspicious gaze on him.

"Elfiné's Holy Sword is useful. I can manipulate it to my ends. Besides, Regina Mercedes is my minion's maid."

"........."

Blackas didn't seem quite convinced, though.

...Ugh, This is so irritating!

Honestly, Leonis didn't know the reason, either, but some part of his heart didn't want to lose those girls.

"I've grown a bit interested in those girls. That is all," Leonis eventually admitted, slightly discouraged.

"...I see. That reason suits you well."

This time, his brother in arms seemed satisfied with his answer. Come to think of it, this wasn't the first time something like this had happened. He'd given Shary a place by his side on a similar sort of whim, even after she'd come to assassinate him.

"You've always been too kind when it comes to your minions, but perhaps this body is making you soft, more humanlike."

"...Impossible." Leonis shook his head bitterly. "Farga!"

He destroyed another bulkhead in his path. The opened passage was infested with writhing tree roots. The miasma filling the air of the tunnel was suffocating.

"Our time for idle talk is at an end, Blackas. It should be straight ahead now."

"Yes..."

Communication with Elfiné had gone completely silent now.

"Uuuuoooooooooooooh...!"

The roots swelled, giving birth to small, animallike Voids.

"Phranis! Phranis! Phranis!"

Leonis used the third-order spell Swift Flame Wave to mercilessly mow down the newly birthed creatures as he rushed the the corridor. Any grand destruction spell that was above the eighth order would likely blow his foes away, but casting such a spell in a closed space like this would bury Leonis alive.

Continuing his advance, the boy eventually came upon a

ruined bulkhead. Behind it lay an enormous opening. Bright, green-tinged light illuminated the space.

"What's that...?" Leonis furrowed his brow the moment he stepped inside.

The source of the light was a massive chunk of mana crystal. Coiled around it were the many roots of the Holy Tree. It was enormous, such that even the portion not enveloped in roots was roughly fifteen meters in diameter.

"I see. So this is the city's power source," Blackas said.

Mana crystals were grown by spirits and ancient gods and, during the era of the Dark Lords' war, served to power the Crag Castle of Dizolf, the Lord of Rage. Nothing but a mana crystal could've powered such a large city. Except...

"I didn't think one this large could form naturally."

"...You don't think this could be man-made, do you?" Leonis whispered.

The two suddenly found themselves interrupted as...

Brrrrrrrrrrrrrrrrrrrrrrrrrrrrrrrrrrrrrrrrrrrrrrrrrrrrrrrrrrrr...

The roots of the Holy Tree began writhing around the mana crystal. They tore through the bulkhead with a loud, quaking sound, sealing Leonis in the chamber. The knots on the roots began swelling, forming countless human faces. Faces, faces, faces—hundreds of them, all resembling wood carvings. Each was an identical visage—the Archsage of the Six Heroes, Arakael Degradios.

"You've fallen quite far, my old nemesis," Leonis observed, tapping the handle of his staff against the ground. "A hero of mankind once lauded as his race's greatest sage is now naught but a seedbed of monsters..."

The Holy Tree's surface was coated with that same black mist. From its body, the tree birthed Voids of different shapes and sizes.

They were the fiends the Archsage had consumed in the war one thousand years ago... And within the tree was Riselia, trapped.

"Now then, Arakael, I'll be taking my minion back." With indomitable confidence, Leonis smirked and began chanting his spell.

CHAPTER 10

THE DEMON SWORD

"Sweep Everything, Flames of Inferno, and Reduce All to Ashes—Zof Amadia!"

Voooooooooooooooooooooooooooosh...!

Not mincing words, Leonis loosed his strongest fire-type spell—the Hellfire Flurry—at the Archsage's many faces. Summoned from the Realm of Muspelheim, the flames immolated the Voids, along with the roots that birthed them.

"Perhaps now you will recall the sheer power of the Undead King, Leonis Death Magnus?"

He tapped hard at the ground with the handle of his Staff of Sealed Sins. The air wavered from the intense heat. The Voids were reduced to cinders, but... The next moment, a dark-green mana flare blinded Leonis. The Holy Tree tore away its scorched appendages and began swiftly regrowing.

"Oh, that's some impressive regeneration. Such is the power of the Holy Tree." The Undead King praised his ancient foe. The Holy Tree of the Spirit Forest grew by sucking up the mana in the ground. Its leaves were a panacea capable of healing any illness, and it was said those who fed on its fruit gained immortality. The Archsage Arakael had tricked the elves of the Spirit Forest in order to make that power his own.

"...Undead... King... Leo...nis..."

The Archsage's faces writhed unnaturally on the tree's surface, calling with strained voices to the boy standing before them.

"Ah, so you can speak. And here I thought you'd completely lost your sentience."

"...I thought you...perished...a thousand years ago..."

"For an Archsage, you're one bloody fool." Leonis sneered. "I would never die. I merely sealed my soul away."

"...The only fool here...is you... The world has...already changed..."

"It certainly has. The food especially has become much more palatable."

The Archsage continued, ignoring Leonis's words as if they'd been nonsense.

"The world shall...be reborn...with the Star of Nothingness..."

"The Star of Nothingness?"

"The Nothingness has chosen me...as herald of the Star's gospel!"

The Archsage's insane laughter echoed through the vast underground tunnel.

"...Look out!" Blackas raised his voice in warning.

"Tch!"

Leaping away, Leonis chanted the eighth-order spell, Multiple Frost Slash—Sharianos.

Blades of frigid ice appeared out of thin air, stabbing into the Holy Tree's roots from every direction. The sharp tendrils smashed through the floor and sped toward Leonis!

"Arooooooooooooooooooooooooooooooo!"

Blackas's body shook as he unleashed his Blast Howl, reducing the roots to dust.

"What's wrong, Leonis?! This isn't like you!"

"...Right."

At Blackas's chiding, Leonis looked down at his hands.

"It seems my mana has weakened greatly."

"What?"

Of course, reverting to his human body was part of it. But it couldn't have been just that. The power of his Zof Amadia spell from earlier and his Sharianos just now...both were significantly weaker than they should have been.

"I get it. It's this place...!" Leonis deduced.

In a manner of speaking, he was inside the Holy Tree's body. The roots strewn everywhere were constantly draining his mana.

"...*Correct, Undead...King...*," the Archsage's voice thundered. "*Become my... Become Arakael Degradios's sustenance...*"

The fruits of immortality on the great tree burst, producing countless Voids of different shapes.

"So what?" Leonis smiled thinly.

"*...What...?*"

"This is a good enough handicap for me, given my opponent is a potted plant that refuses to die."

Leonis lifted his staff, and the presence of death quickly surrounded him. The shadow at his feet expanded at once and rang out with the eerie sound of clattering bones.

"Personal sorcery—Create Undead Legion!"

An army of skeletons erupted from his shadow, each holding a weapon that shone with magical energy.

Clack, click, creak, clack...

A veritable hill of bones surged from beneath Leonis's feet. From atop it, Leonis lorded over the flock of Voids. The scene had become something of an accurate reenactment of the battle of the Wasteland of Sidon, a thousand years past.

"My army of loyal undead...," Leonis commanded boldly. "Overrun my foolish foe!"

The mountain of bones clacked and creaked as it surged forward like a wave.

◆

Leo...?

Riselia's consciousness awakened within the darkness... She thought she'd heard his voice.

"...!"

The girl tried moving, but vines coiled tightly around her body, rendering her immobile.

Right, that tree caught me after we defeated a Void...

And that was how she'd lost consciousness. Her field of vision was dark, and she couldn't see anything. The harder she tried to struggle, the harder the vines gripped and constricted her. And on top of it all, the rotten miasma the Voids produced suffused the air around her. If she weren't already undead, it surely would have rotted her lungs from the inside.

"...Let go of me...!"

She bit into the vines with her sharp fangs but couldn't tear through them.

...What do I do...?

Even if she summoned her Holy Sword, it wouldn't help her if she couldn't move. But then...

"—lia...hear me...?"

The boy's voice shook her eardrums.

"Leo...?!"

The comms device hanging off one of her ears lit up, but the boy's voice cut out just as quickly as it had emerged. Leonis was coming to save her... That alone gave her strength. Back on the surface, Regina and Sakuya were likely fighting hard, too.

That's right... If I don't fight now, why did I even awaken power of a Holy Sword in the first place?!

A faint glow began radiating from Riselia's silver hair.

◆

Leonis tightened his grasp on the earring-type communication device. Riselia gave no response. He couldn't tell if his voice had reached her or not, but he knew she was in there. There was no doubting it.

The demonic wolf prince of the Realm of Shadows sailed across the bones as if surfing over surging waves.

"Dark Dragon of Flames, Devour My Foes—Jirus Vera!"

Riding on his sworn friend's back, Leonis chanted a sixth-order spell. Black flames of darkness took the shape of a dragon and devoured the Voids. It was one of the Undead King's unique, personal spells. Its magic kneaded the elements of death and flames into one. Black fire ran wild, eating into the immortal Holy Tree as an army of skeleton soldiers continued their advance.

"...*Chant a hymn...of light...*"

Countless faces of an old man surfaced on the trunk of the Holy Tree, all of them reciting the same words at once.

"...It's using sorcery?!" Leonis's eyes widened.

Arakael was trying to chant a high-order spell of holy magic. Moreover, it was a multi-person chant, done through his countless faces.

...*Like the Holy Sect's priests.*

The priests under Arakael's command had likely been fused into the tree as well. Leonis had no way of knowing if they had been forced or had willingly sacrificed their bodies for the sake of the Six Heroes...

Regardless, a massive spell circle shone, suspended in the air. It was an eighth-order holy spell—the Divine Light Cannon, Lex Megido.

Flashes of light rained down like lightning, smiting the army of undead. Skeletons that took a direct hit were reduced to cinders immediately, and even the spell's shock waves were enough to rob the skeletons of their pseudo-life, returning them to mere bones.

"Blackas!"

The great wolf leapt in response to Leonis's command, weaving between the blades of holy light. The two closed in on the Holy Tree.

"Darkness, Burst Forth—Arzam!" Leonis chanted a tenth-order spell.

Black flames combusted from thin air, striking the Holy Tree. But the enormous plant merely generated new faces to replace the ones that had been destroyed. The new ones quickly resumed their chanting. A barrier of light dropped like a curtain, repelling the darkness and erasing Leonis's spell.

Arakael had cast a defensive spell—the Sacred Barrier, Ras Gu Roa.

It can conjure an eighth-order and seventh-order spell at the same time...

Leonis clicked his tongue as he landed on the ground. He could do that much, too, of course. But the fact that it could still use sorcery like that, even after having lost so much intelligence...

"I see. It's no wonder they called you Archsage," Leonis said with an ironic smirk.

"Such a large amount of mana. It even exceeds the amounts he had when he was alive, does it not?" Blackas asked.

"Yes..." The Undead Lord gave a short nod. "He's probably absorbing mana directly from that huge mana crystal."

Arakael effectively had an inexhaustible source of mana, enabling him to chant multiple spells at once. By comparison, Leonis's mana was being depleted just by his presence there.

...I'll be at a disadvantage if this battle lingers for too long.

Arakael, on the other hand, had fused with the Holy Tree and was immortal. He would be able to almost instantly recover from any average spell. And so long as he lived, he could produce an endless supply of Voids.

This place was an altar. An altar of blood, prepared for the purpose of slaying Leonis as a sacrifice.

Le...o...ni...iiiiiiiiiiiiiiiissssssssss...!

The dead consumed by the Holy Tree howled. There was no awareness to their wails. All Leonis could hear was hunger. Roots swung down to strike at the child, but he repelled them with a sequence of gravity spells.

A high-scale destruction spell might be able to annihilate this entire area.

But that would also destroy the mana crystal powering the Assault Garden. Riselia would be caught in the blast, too...

My minion, eh...?

Then Leonis hit upon an idea.

It'll be a gamble...

The Undead King tightened his grip on the earring device and said:

"Blackas. I'm going to try something reckless."

"Reckless, hmm? Very well. I am the prince of the Realm of Shadows, after all."

The huge black wolf shook his body. He was Leonis's irreplaceable brother in arms who had run at his side across countless battlefields. Even with no further explanation, the wolf could tell what Leonis was thinking.

Again, Leonis began an incantation, summoning a legion of the undead.

"Armies of the undead, follow my lead...!"

The troops let out an enthusiastic, clattering cry as they followed Leonis's charge.

◆

"I won't lose...! Won't...lose...!"

Mana lit up Riselia's silvery hair as she tore off the vines of the Holy Tree and began crawling her way out. The more she struggled, the harder the vines dug into her skin, leaving bleeding lacerations all over her body. Even so, Riselia persisted...

"Let goooooooooooooooooooooooooo!"

She wouldn't lose. She wouldn't, wouldn't, wouldn't, wouldn't...!

"I absolutely won't lose...!"

On that day six years ago, the Third Assault Garden was overrun by Voids, and her parents were killed. On that day, she had sworn:

...I don't want to be someone who's always waiting to be rescued...!

The girl's blood surged; that seething, hot fluid gathered and became a blade of unrivaled sharpness. It sliced through the vines binding her limbs.

◆

Uuuuooooooooooooooooooooooooooooooooooooooooooh!

Countless magic circles appeared, surrounding Leonis and

Blackas. The fires of the eighth-order holy magic, Divine Light Cannon, consumed the army of skeletons. Standing atop the mountain of toppled bones, Leonis rushed forward atop the back of his black wolf companion. A giant-class Void rose up from beneath the rubble, swinging its humongous fist down in an attempt to crush them both.

"Gran Beld!"

Firing a Heavy Destruction Blast, a seventh-order gravity spell, he knocked the Void's massive body to the ground, sending stone flying into the air. Shards of rock skimmed across his face, leaving streaks of blood trailing down his skin.

The tree's roots sprang into action. Countless faces appeared on their tips, chanting holy magic. Yet another Divine Light Cannon.

"Blackas!"

Leonis jumped off the black wolf's back, thrusting the tip of his staff against the Holy Tree. Blackas Shadow Prince's body became as shadow and coiled around Leonis's arm as he swung. This was another of Leonis's personal spells—Howling Blaze!

The black wolf's head howled. Surrounded with massive amounts of mana, the beast tore through the pack of Voids and bit into the faces appearing on the trunk of the Holy Tree. Leonis's and Arakael's mana collided, crashing into each other.

But Leonis only had a human body's worth of mana, while Arakael had a mana crystal capable of powering a city at his disposal. The difference in their capacities was as stark as that of heaven and earth. Leonis was only able to keep up because he was the proud Undead King, he who'd mastered the arcane arts.

...Where are you?

Leonis strained his eyes, trying to look into the writhing depths of the Holy Tree. He scanned every inch, searching for his minion among the suffocating, blinding amounts of mana... And then he found it: an intense concentration of magical energy.

"...There you are!"

Leonis closed one of his eyes, extended his left hand forward... and flicked his thumb.

"Ii Ray!"

The Lightning Flash spell used electricity to propel blades forward at high speeds—it was an assassination technique. However, he hadn't launched a blade; it was Riselia's communication earring. The accessory was fairly aerodynamically shaped, though launching something like that with the spell had no chance of actually damaging Arakael.

"...Is that your...last resort...Undead King...?"

The faces on the tree's stump cackled manically.

"Laugh all you want. The only fool here is you, Archsage," Leonis retorted confidently.

It was then that a sudden crack ran through the Holy Tree's massive, regenerating trunk.

Creeeaaaaak, snap!

Bloodred light seeped through the fissures, eating up the Holy Tree from the inside.

"What...? What did you...? What did you doooooooooooooooo?!" The faces on the tree's trunk contorted in pain.

"Oh, I simply shared some of my blood and mana with my minion."

The Holy Tree's surface cracked, and then...burst open. A flurry of long silver hair spread like wings of magical light.

"Leo!"

The Vampire Queen—Riselia Crystalia. Her eyes shone a brilliant shade of crimson.

She's awakened to her vampiric power...!

The sight of her spreading her mana wings to fly above and lord over that which lay below was breathtakingly beautiful.

"Leo... Aaaah, aaaah?!"

But then, unaccustomed as she was to her new magical appendages, she gave them a flap and went into an awkward tailspin.

...She still isn't used to using her mana wings.

With the support of Leonis's floating magic, she landed at his side.

"I see you've learned how to use your vampire powers."

"Yes. This is your blood, isn't it...?"

Riselia opened her hands, revealing a blood-smeared earring. It was indeed Leonis's blood, charged with massive amounts of mana.

"That was just the trigger. Your mana was already overflowing as it was, Selia."

Leonis knew she was on the verge of awakening within the Holy Tree. He simply gave her his blood to serve as the catalyst for the explosion.

"Do you need more?" Leonis extended his finger toward her, prompting Riselia to blush.

"I—I got plenty already!"

The young woman then turned and faced the Holy Tree as it continued screaming in agony.

"So that's the Void Lord...," she said, her expression stiff with discomfort at the monstrosity's unnatural appearance. "It regrows so fast... How are we going to stop it...?"

"Selia, could you buy me some time?"

"Huh?"

"I'll wipe it out, completely."

Riselia appeared to doubt whether Leonis was truly capable of such a feat, but she concealed her concern. Leonis gave an assured smile and tightened his grip on his staff.

"It'll take me a while to do it, so protect me until then."

"...Understood." She nodded, her voice full of trust.

Riselia then raised one hand into the air.

"Activate!"

With that, a crimson blade formed between her fingers. She ran it across her arm, as if playing a stringed instrument. Blood dripped down as she cut her flesh; the red liquid pooled at her feet as she winced from the pain.

"What are you doing?"

"I'll show you how this Holy Sword is used...!"

Uuuuuuooooooooooooooooooooooooooooooooooooooooooooooh!

A group of newly born giant-class Voids charged toward them. Riselia drove her crimson, bloodstained blade into the ground. The next moment, the blood pooling on the floor rose up, coalescing into a number of floating blades.

"This is my Holy Sword—the Bloody Sword!" Riselia spoke the weapon's name proudly.

The blades of blood rushed forward, slicing the advancing Voids to ribbons.

...It has the ability to protect its wielder automatically?!

A Holy Sword is a reflection of its wielder's soul, and this one's ability allowed it to manipulate blood... A most fitting ability for a girl who'd become a Vampire Queen.

"I'll protect you, Leo!"

Countless flowers of blood bloomed.

"...I see. You've found a truly skilled minion," Blackas said, surfacing from Leonis's shadow.

"Yes. Like I thought, she's worthy of being my right-hand woman," the boy replied with a smile.

And now, as her master, he would have to respond to his minion's efforts in kind. He would destroy the Archsage Arakael with the dignity of an Undead King. There was no need to hold back now that his servant was safe.

Playtime was officially over.

Leonis twisted the hilt of his staff lightly, and it fell heavily to the ground.

The staff concealed a sword within.

An overwhelming surge of mana rushed forth the moment the weapon was unsheathed.

"Wh-what...? What is this...?!" demanded the innumerable faces etched into the Holy Tree.

The Holy Tree, the mighty Archsage, was afraid. Leonis slowly stepped forward.

"Leo?!" Riselia exclaimed.

"A certain envious goddess once told me not to go around drawing this sword needlessly..."

The Staff of Sealed Sins was a legend-class artifact, but in truth, it was just a scabbard for the mythology-class weapon it concealed.

The Undead King Leonis had only ever wielded this sword twice. The first time, he reduced the mountain that was home to the massive Sacred Dragon to scorched earth...

The second time, he slew a god.

Uuuuuuuooooooooooooooooooooooooooooooooooooooooooooh!

The massive mana crystal filled with light. The Holy Tree was preparing to cast the tenth-order spell Providence Annihilation—Aion. It intended to destroy everything surrounding it altogether. This was the core of the Assault Garden, and if this place was destroyed, the whole city would collapse. Perhaps Arakael was confident the Holy Tree would survive with its immortality.

...No, that thing probably doesn't have enough intelligence to understand that much anymore.

Leonis heaved a sigh of exasperation and brandished his sword. The blade gleamed with darkness.

This was the holy sword given to the greatest swordsman among the Six Heroes, Leonis. A holy sword...? No, the blessing of the Goddess had reforged it into a demon sword—one kept sealed so as to contain its intense power...

Thou Art the Sword to Save the World, Gifted by the Heavens.

Thou Art the Sword to Ruin the World, Made to Rebel Against the Heavens.

A Holy Sword, Sanctified by the Gods.

A Demon Sword, Blessed by the Goddess.

I Demarcate This Land as My Kingdom and Wield You to Lay Waste to My Foes.

Let Your Name, Submerged in Darkness, Ring Forth—

"The Demon Sword, Dáinsleif!"

The Demon Sword glinted in the light as Leonis readied its black blade. It was the antithesis of a holy sword. It had been blessed by the Goddess who rebelled against the gods of the Celestial Sphere. And since it was wielded by a Dark Lord, it became known as the Demon Sword.

However, Dáinsleif still retained its will from when it was a Holy Sword and was sealed so it could only be drawn under a very specific condition. And that condition was...

To protect one's kingdom.

Dáinsleif was originally forged to protect one's country. A weapon for safeguarding one's kingdom and driving away invaders...

And so the Undead King proclaimed this land, the Seventh Assault Garden, as his kingdom. He declared the citizens on the surface to be his subjects and Excalibur Academy to be the castle over which he reigned. The fact that he successfully drew the Demon Sword meant it acknowledged this as Leonis's domain.

It was entirely unexpected and unplanned, but from this moment forward, the Seventh Assault Garden and Excalibur Academy would have to become the base for the resurgence of the Dark Lords' Armies. And this Void Lord who threatened the lives of his subjects was...

"You are the enemy I am meant to strike down," Leonis decreed, resolute. He gripped the Demon Sword in his hands.

...Impossible... Why do you possess...the Holy Sword that struck down a god...?

The fearful voices of the Archsage reverberated through the underground tunnel.

"...Oh? Have you regained enough of your sentience to know fear?" Leonis sneered for a moment before vanishing from where he stood.

"Leo?!" Riselia raised her voice in surprise.

The Goddess of Rebellion had sealed more than just the Demon Sword's power in the blade. She'd also sealed within the weapon Leonis's power and experience from when he was a hero. Which meant that when Leonis held the Demon Sword, he would regain the power of the greatest swordsman to have ever lived.

The master of the Demon Sword cut through the assembled Voids in the blink of an eye and leaped high into the air. The Archsage's faces twisted and contorted grotesquely on the trunk of the Holy Tree.

"Any last words, king of the Voids...?"

...Ruin...cannot be overturned... No matter what...

"I am the Undead King. Destiny is governed by my hand," Leonis said with a scoff, and then...

"Secret Blade Art of the Rognas Kingdom School—Ragna Lost!"

The Demon Sword's blade unleashed an incredible black light, eradicating the Holy Tree from existence.

"Roselia! No! Why...why are you...?!"

"Don't cry, Leonis."

She extended a hand. Even as it was being eaten away by nothingness, she gave him a kindly smile.

"A thousand years from now, I will be reborn."

She pleaded for Leonis to find her, no matter the cost...

"...I promise! No matter what, I'll find you, Roselia!"

Thus, the girl known as the Goddess of Rebellion offered him a final, fleeting smile.

◆

With the Void Lord's destruction, the Stampede came to an end. Having lost their commander, the Voids grew sluggish and were taken out one after another by the Holy Swordsmen of Excalibur Academy. The Voids' carcasses were piled on top of one another and eventually dissolved into mist. They left no bodies behind, disappearing into the emptiness that was their namesake...

At Excalibur Academy's Hræsvelgr dorm, Leonis spent half the day lying in bed in Riselia's room.

...Blast it all... The feared and lauded Undead King...suffering from muscle pains...

This was the recoil from wielding the power he'd held as a swordsman that had been sealed within Dáinsleif. His untrained, ten-year-old body was stricken with crippling muscle pain. It felt as if his every tendon had been torn.

And it even took all my mana away... What an absurd Demon Sword.

With little else to do, Leonis staved off his boredom by watching movies. The entertainment of this era was far more interesting than the theater of a thousand years ago. At first, he took what movies he could find in the library, but finishing those, he decided to watch selections from Riselia's collection. Most of them were love stories between a noble and a commoner, with a few rather passionate scenes.

...So she likes these sorts of stories. I'm a bit surprised.

Leonis rolled about on the bed as that thought circulated in his mind.

"Leo, I brought you lunch... Wait, wh-wh-wh-what are you doing...?!"

Riselia had returned to the room and, upon noticing what was playing on the screen, reacted in a flustered panic.

"Y-you can't watch that! It's too soon for you, Leo!"

She grabbed the screen's control device and promptly turned off the film.

"...I was just getting to the best part..." Leonis frowned.

"No. If you want to watch a movie, you have the ones Sakuya lent you."

"But they're uninteresting..."

Those movies were of men with katanas in hand trying to cut

each other. They were rather brutal and hardly suited Leonis's taste. He'd seen enough violence a thousand years ago and preferred to watch something a bit more peaceful and healing for his amusement.

Riselia sat down on the bed.

"They started rebuilding the commercial district, but it looks like it'll take some time to fix the broken power system. We'll have to stay in this part of the ocean for a while."

"I see..."

"Also, the news reported that the Void Lord died naturally after awakening in an incomplete state."

Her expression seemed a bit discontent, as if to say, "even though you were the one who defeated it."

"That's fine. I'd prefer it if my identity wasn't exposed anyway," Leonis said.

But his words prompted intense scrutiny from Riselia.

"Just who are you, really?" she asked.

"I told you already. An ancient sorcerer who was sealed away and then reawakened."

"But you used a sword."

".........." Leonis averted his gaze.

"...Well, fine." She shrugged. "Here. The orphanage's owner, Phrenia, told me to give you this."

"...Mmm?"

She took a small flower-shaped decoration out of her shawl.

"What's this?"

"A medal. The kids at the orphanage made it for you."

It was a clumsily shaped blue flower, constructed from paper.

"...A medal, eh?" Leonis found himself smirking bitterly.

He'd declared this place the Undead King's kingdom, but that didn't matter right now.

Anyone who pays respect to the Undead King is worthy of protection...

Just then...

"...B-by the way, Leo..." Riselia fidgeted, her face flaring pink.

"What is it?"

"Erm, actually, I, uhhh, when I use my Holy Sword, I deplete a lot of my blood..."

"Oh... Yes, I assume you would."

Its power was to turn her blood into blades, after all.

"So I, um... I really want some..."

"Didn't you say you'd be patient and endure it?"

"...You bully..."

At Leonis's exasperated question, tears welled up in Riselia's eyes.

Her face was flushed, and she eyed him with a pained, longing expression.

"...Fine. Just a little, though." Leonis nodded.

Whispering an "I'm sorry," Riselia brought her lips to Leonis's neck, and...

"Lady Selia, how's the kid doin—? Wait, whaaaaaaaaaaaaaaat?!"

Regina walked into the room without knocking and gaped at them with wide eyes.

"...Aaah, R-Regina?!"

"We came to visit the kid while he was feeling down, but..." Sakuya, who had also walked in, turned around while pretending not to have seen anything. "Sorry. Looks like you were in the middle of something."

"L-Lady Selia, what are you doing to him?!"

"...This isn't what you think! This is, erm... I'm nursing him back to health! Yes, I'm taking care of him, and..."

"Hmm, Selia? I'm pretty sure this is in violation of dorm

regulations...," Elfiné, having also made her entrance, said with a conflicted expression.

"Miss Elfiné, you've got this all wrong!"

Shrugging tiredly at the riot going on around him, Leonis turned his gaze out the window. Voids, Holy Swords, and the words left behind by the resurrected member of the Six Heroes.

"The world shall be reborn with the Star of Nothingness..." Hmm...

Was it just the Archsage's nonsensical babble as he lost his mind to the Voids?

Regardless of whether it's true or not, I must hurry and rebuild the Dark Lords' Armies...

Looking out the window at the damage Excalibur Academy had suffered, he considered what was to come, not yet aware that this was but a prelude to the tumultuous days ahead...

Taking a bath with a Dark Lord is all right if he's ten, right...?

Hello, everyone, this is Yu Shimizu. It's a pleasure to meet any of my first-time readers, and to those who've read my previous series, *Blade Dance of Elementalers*, it's been two months or so since my last publication.

Thank you all for waiting. This is my new series for the new Reiwa era in Japan, *The Demon Sword Master of Excalibur Academy*! The greatest Dark Lord, the Undead King, is reborn after one thousand years—only to find he's now a ten-year-old boy! Sorcery has declined and disappeared, with a world of developed magitech taking its place. It's a sword fantasy where he's surrounded by cute older girls!

How did you like it? To sum up the concept of this work, it is the appearance of a child and the intellect of a Dark Lord! Maybe it sounds similar to some other work of fiction, hmm?

He possesses the power of the greatest Dark Lord, but at the same time, he looks like a boy who's only ten years old. Please look forward to finding out what meetings and battles await our Dark Lord Leonis at Excalibur Academy!

Now then, I'd like to offer some thanks.

Firstly, to Asagi Tosaka, for drawing the illustrations for this volume. Thank you very much! As you can surely see, dear readers, they can only be summed up as: the best!

I knew how detailed and subtle your designs were from *Girly Air Force*, but you gave the characters a sense of presence and cuteness that exceeded my expectations. That includes the school uniforms!

To my editors, my editor in chief, proofreaders, designers, and the printing office. I've really caused you a great deal of trouble this time around. This was the tightest schedule I've had to adhere to as an author, but thanks to all of you, I've managed to get the book published. My deepest gratitude.

And lastly, to you readers of my story. Thank you very much! Thankfully, it's already been decided that the series will continue. I'll do my best to deliver the next volume as soon as possible, and I'd be happy if you could show your support for the series then.

A small taste of what the next volume will include! The Undead King Leonis finally begins his school life in earnest. Riselia worries over having become a [redacted]. Elfiné takes up an unusual job. Shary and Regina have a gyoza-making standoff. And the young love of little Tessera (age eight) develops. Please look forward to it!

Yu Shimizu, April 2019

Thank you for picking up The Demon Sword Master of Excalibur Academy! I put my all into expressing the cuteness and coolness of the characters. Nothing would make me happier than knowing you enjoyed the story and the illustrations....!

ASAGI TOSAKA